A Woman who Lives by the Sea

In the creative hotbed of 1960s London, strong-willed American stage-designer Susie Conrad married a suave English actor and took the West End by storm. Many years later, her unexpected rescue of stranded holidaymakers turns her isolated home on the Northumbrian coast into an arena for re-awakened passions and for a re-assessment of her life as artist, wife and lover. This novel, both frank and lyrical, explores a woman's quest for love, independence and fulfilment with honesty and realism.

This new edition of *A Woman who Lives by the Sea* is dedicated *in memoriam* to my mother Dinkie who was first to introduce me to the great curving beach at Embleton and to actress Maxine Howe who was first to bring this story alive in her superb performance. They are no longer with us but are remembered with love on the beautiful Northumbrian coast and within these pages.

A Woman who Lives by the Sea

And did you never lie upon the shore
And watch the curl'd white
of the coming wave
Glass'd in the slippery sand
before it breaks?

From 'A Dream of Fair Women'
by Alfred, Lord Tennyson.

1 The Sea

I am a woman who lives by the sea. At least I am in Summer: that's when I come up here to the North of England and open up my little house above the beach. Sometimes the dawn comes up cool and gray with only a faint pink promise of the day ahead. Sometimes there'll be mist, and even my creaking this door open and slamming back the shutters won't break the silence; everything is swallowed into vast blankness and I'll stand barefoot on the wet planks here, listening to the faintly swishing sea. Sometimes it will be bright and blue and I'll feel the warm dry wood under my toes; that's when I see the whole great curving beach laid out beneath me with the little island at one end, the seaweed moved into new places by the tide, and the gulls soaring up over the dunes. But however it may look under different lights, every morning I'll come out here on to my verandah and renew my love of the place.

It's a big change from London, where I still live in the Winter, but it does remind me just a bit of the place I grew up with my kid sister in Maine. She hated the sea though, and couldn't wait to go to College, get married, and move out West with that farmer of hers. Me? I went to New York full of dreams to be a dancer—huh, but I was too big and my back hurt! So they gave me a job painting the scenery, would you believe? I got to Broadway though, and pretty soon I wasn't just painting those damn sets, I was designing them. Then there were a few years when all the big-shot producers wanted sets by Susie Conrad. It was fun. I met the big stars and went to the parties and there I'd be, somewhere down on the bottom left of the bill: 'Designed by Susie Conrad'. I enjoyed all that, I won't deny it, and I enjoyed the money, but the best thing was making dreams into reality: my dreams and other people's dreams. I know that's a corny line, but I believe that's what art and entertainment should be all about. If you can't dream, you shouldn't be in showbusiness. Well, I was proud to be a maker of dreams. Call it phony if you like, but I loved it and was fulfilled by it.

It had to end of course, when a new generation came up from nowhere and took over — the way new generations do. Suddenly I was old-fashioned. So I married an English actor, we came to London, and I did some work in the English theatre — some of it very good, I have to say. But Jack was an alcoholic — Susie sure can pick 'em — and the whole thing went on the rocks. It all seems so long ago. Don't get me wrong, I'm not bitter. I loved Jack and wanted to marry him even though I knew he was a drunk. I wasn't stupid enough to think I could change him, but I really loved him and wanted to be with him all the time and thought I could cope. Well, I got what I bargained for...only more. The lies, the deceit, the stupid arguments with me apologizing for Jack all the time in front of our friends, the waking up to a bedful of shit: you can only take so much of that. I couldn't manage Jack any more, and the truth is I didn't want to. I certainly couldn't stop him drinking…so we were divorced and I'm not sorry. He's getting a lot of TV work now as an older character actor. You know the kinda thing: playing prosperous businessmen, colonels, senior policemen, that kinda role. He's very good, but God knows how they wipe him down and get him on the set on time. Still, that's not my problem any more: there'll be some poor sucker of a glamour-girl doing it for him. He always was attractive to women.

So, when that was all over and I'd found out who my real friends were (Jilly, are you reading this book? You're a saint!), one of them got me a job with a touring theater company and I really saw England for the first time. All those depressing towns! But get up to the North here—we're nearly into Scotland—and the countryside is really something. This North-East coast is just wonderful: so quiet and beautiful. Once I'd seen it on a day-trip out from Newcastle, I just wanted to keep coming back and not tell anyone in case they brought the crowds! Then I found this house and bought it right away. Some people say I'm crazy to live in a shack on a beach in the North of England, but they don't know this place and what it's done for me.

So every morning I'm here I'll come outside, push back the shutters, lean on the verandah railing and look out across the sea. I'll watch the people as they come along the beach: there's Jennie from the stables, exercising one of the racehorses; she's always out early. Later I might see Patrick the birdwatcher; he'll always give me a wave. Then when the day gets going there'll be families who come for picnics and kids playing at the edge of the water. It's usually too cold for swimming and it's certainly no sunbather's beach, except on those few baking-hot days when the whole world seems to stand still and the place shimmers like a dream. But whoever walks the sand, the sea is always there; the people make no difference to that, nor to me. I can watch them come and go in their sweet ignorance of my life. What can they know of me and why should they care? If they see me at all, I'm just a woman who lives by the sea. But once, only once, two people did make a difference — on one of those baking-hot days when the whole world seemed to stand still and the place shimmered like a dream.

* * *

I had come out a little earlier than usual that morning and was opening up the house. It was brilliantly sunny and warm even at that hour and the whole place was lit up under a clear blue sky. I noticed right away it was high tide, the sea very calm, not a ship in sight, larks singing up from the dunes behind me: a beautiful morning, a wonderful morning. I stood at the rail with my coffee just taking it all in…and that was when I noticed two people on the island.

It's a very little island, just off the point at the Northern end of the beach; more what you'd call an islet: less than two hundred yards long, very flat and rocky but with a high point at one end, a cleft of grass in the middle and a miniature bay on the seaward side. It's a natural draw to visitors, especially kids who want to go exploring, and at low tide it's easy to explore: you just walk out over the sand and the rocks. But at high tide it's completely cut off by three hundred yards of water — and I quickly realized that is what these two had discovered. They must have been stuck on the island for half the night. Even at this distance I could see they were agitated: one of them was pacing about, the other waving both arms up and down in that instinctive attention-grabbing distress signal. I went inside for my binoculars. I could see them plainly through the glasses: a girl of about twenty in jeans and a blue-and-white-striped sailor's jersey, and man who looked the same age wearing a white zip-up jacket. She was the one doing the waving. She would stop now and again to run fingers through her tousled blonde hair. The man was walking up and down the island's shore looking glumly at the water. It was clear that neither of them had seen me, for they were both directing their attention to the village, more than a mile distant around the point. My house is in the dunes but quite conspicuous and they must have noticed it. If they really wanted to attract attention all they had to do was turn round and they would see me — but possibly they thought the house was empty and that their best hopes of rescue lay in the village. It was natural enough to think so, but I knew that no-one would be likely to see them from that distance or to take much notice if they did. They could risk an early morning wetting, wait for the tide to go down, or get me to help.

I studied them through the binoculars, smiling to myself. They'd likely be holidaymakers who had wandered on to the island, stayed too long, and gotten caught—without the sense or courage simply to wade off. Even now the water would scarcely be chest-high, but of course they wouldn't know that. They surely were prize fools, especially to have gotten caught overnight. I smiled again as I silently gave them the Embarrassed Couple of the Year Award for Worst Holiday Mistake. Of *course* it was their own fault! They could keep on blaming each other...I thought I could see them doing it from here...no way off without getting wet and looking stupid...or they could just look this way and their nice Auntie Susie would wave to them and start the rescue and Thunderbirds would be Go and it would be a home run. Then I smiled even more: they were young, handsome and pretty. Maybe they were lovers. Maybe they'd had more fun on that island than I knew about. But this morning I guessed the fun was over. She looked anxious; he looked sore. They moved like figures from a dream across my hazy, magnified view...and I was visited by the realization that I held them in my power: not merely through these binoculars that let me snoop unobserved on their every movement, but in a real and physical sense. It was in my power to let them wait or to effect a quick and surprising rescue. It didn't occur to me to wonder who they were or to speculate too much on their lives outside this predicament, but—as I smiled again behind the glasses—I did wonder what they would make of me if we met, and how narrowly they would have missed me if I chose to leave them. Held in my magnified vision, they had somehow become my responsibility.

I put down the binoculars, stepped forward off the verandah and yelled "Hey there!" They didn't hear me. I waved furiously. "Hey! Hi there!" My voice broke the morning calm and they both turned to raise their arms and acknowledge me. "It's okay!" I yelled. "I'm on my way!" Maybe they wouldn't be able to distinguish all my words but I felt

I had to shout something. As I started down the sandy slope to the beach, I saw the girl jump up and down with what I took to be joy and relief.

Warm, dry, powdery sand whispered between my toes; my blue skirt billowed up. What would they think of me, running to their rescue? Then I was down on the beach; the sand was cold and damp and cracking under my heels as I turned and gave them another wave as if to say 'Just a minute, I have to go this way first.' They were watching me scamper out of sight and I sensed that all our hearts were beating faster. None of it was truly necessary; I was making a drama out of nothing. But then I thought: there is always drama on this beach. The merest stirring of a rock-pool can be just as significant as the wildest storm — or two strangers on the island. I was running needlessly into their lives in this hectic moment, but I was also running through my own life and through the life of this place.

I got to my boat: the tiny fiberglass bathtub of a boat I use for rowing off the rocks or paddling around the bay when it is calm enough. I associated my little boat with idle pleasures, but now I unchained the oars, dragged her down the beach and splashed aboard with a new purpose. In a few moments I was rowing across the still water. They watched me coming, their hands in their pockets, and moved down to the water's edge.

"Hello!" I shouted when I was within easy hailing-distance. "I'll get you off. I saw you were stuck. The other side!" I pointed. "The far shore!" I knew a place where the water would be deep enough for me to come in astern to some flat rocks. They'd never even get their feet wet. I rowed around to the other side of the island and backed in. The boat bumped against the rocks. The girl came forward first, on canvas shoes.

"Watch that rock," I warned. "It's slippery."

"This is very good of you,"

said the man, picking up a small backpack I hadn't noticed. "We didn't fancy being marooned for half the day."

"It's no trouble; really it isn't. Are you on holiday?"

"Yes we are, " answered the girl, stepping into the boat and clambering past me. "It's so lucky you saw us." She was young, good-looking with a fine nose and bright hair and she smelled of perfume.

"Oh, I see most things. My house is just up there. That's right, you sit behind me. Now you go in the stern. Uh-huh, that's it."

The boat rocked as the man took his seat. With three people aboard, it settled very low in the water. I pulled away gently from the island, learning the boat's new weight and summing up my passengers. The girl was asking me where I lived and how I had seen them. She was obviously relieved to have been taken off, but the man was embarrassed by the rescue. I smiled at him; caught him looking self-consciously at my wet bare feet, my brown hands on

18

the oars, the brightly-colored scarf at my neck, my short hair. He was dark and rather glum-looking. He had missed a shave. He felt he had to speak.

"We've put you to terrible trouble."

"Don't say that. I enjoy an early morning row. We're lucky it's calm; three's too many for this little boat."

"It's enormously good of you."

He was young and modern but still spoke with the traditional good manners of the English gentleman.

"That's okay. Were you out there all night?"

"Most of the night, yes." The girl spoke hurriedly before the man had time to answer. "We actually fell asleep there just when it was getting dark."

"We woke up to find ourselves cut off," added the man, looking past me to the girl.

"Lucky it's Summer," I said. "Spring storms sweep right over that island, and in Winter you'd surely freeze."

"Well," the girl answered with even more relief in her voice, "it was very good of you to get your boat out especially for us."

"No trouble. It's been some excitement for me. And don't worry, I'm not some crazy tourist; despite my voice I really do live here." We were heading in now. "Really," I went on, "you could have waded off: it's not so deep, but I guess the boat ride's more fun for you." I shipped the oars, the boat grounded on the beach, both my passengers swayed nervously as she stuck on the sand. "D'you want to come in for breakfast?"

"Yes please," said the girl, "we'd like that very much—if it's not more trouble for you."

"No trouble."

I stepped into the cold water and helped them jump on to dry sand.

"Are your legs not freezing in that water?" squealed the girl. "I've needed my wellies every day on this trip."

"No, I'm strictly a barefoot girl: no shoes for me here unless it's seriously cold or I'm going shopping in the village; sometimes not even then. Don't you know it feels good to go barefoot? You should try it."

"Not today thanks," she giggled.

"Well, you must be tough," remarked the man, watching the clear water round my bare legs...or was he watching my bare legs in the clear water? Time was when I was real proud of my legs. "How cold is the sea here?"

"*Very* cold," I grinned, "but it freshens you up."

After the boat had been hauled back up the beach we trailed through the dunes in single file. These two were thin on conversation. In silence we brushed through the sharp marram grass, listened to the morning skylarks, and felt the first real warmth of the sun.

"Looks to me it's going to be a fine day, " I told them, stopping and pointing back to the island. "See that?" Now, from this height in the dunes, they could see exactly where they had been and just how shallow the water was between the island and the shore. "You couldn't have come to any real harm."

"Thanks anyway." The man smiled his relief at me, as if he had regained a confidence and a friendliness with dry land. We came up to the house. As always, the short grass with its daisies and clover had brushed the sand quite naturally from my feet; they felt they had to stamp it off their shoes. "You live here all alone?"

"In Summer I do. The village is just around the bay there — but it is very quiet and that's how I like it."

"So you're an American," he observed pointlessly. There was something very attractive in his clipped voice, even when stating the annoyingly obvious.

"Well, is that still a capital offence in this country?"

"No, I just wondered..." He was taking no pleasure in verbal sparring and it would have been rude of me to continue the match. "I just wondered if you, how you..."

"Like I said, I live here. I've lived in England since I was quite young. This is my Summer house; I've got a place in London for Winter."

"It's a wonderful little house," said the girl. "You *are* lucky."

"Come in, please. D'you want porridge, or just coffee? I could boil some eggs."

The man chuckled.

"I don't think I've had porridge since I was at school."

"You should have porridge—it's good."

"I think we'll have the eggs, thank you," said the girl, "and the coffee."

I opened the door and ushered them in. They looked briefly round the main room and sat at the table, intrigued by my house: its tiny wooden proportions, the eccentricities of my comfortable life inside it. As I went into the kitchen I realized I had strangers in my house: the first strangers I had ever had in this house.

"Okay now." I set the stove

going. "Mother will feed her newly-acquired grown-up family. You can tell me about yourselves if you want — or if you just want to eat, that's fine."

"Can we help?" asked the girl.

"Certainly not. You're my guests. Guests are rare and special creatures here."

It came to me that they smelled: not strongly or unpleasantly, but with a damp and oddly-perfumed odor of an urban life that was no longer mine. Although I could see them sitting quite easily at the table and looking out of the window, I was acutely aware of being watched and studied as I moved around. I was an unexpected curiosity I their lives as much as they were an event in mine. But the self-consciousness seemed to be all my own: they had relaxed into my little house and watched me bring them boiled eggs and coffee as if I were indeed that mother feeding a family.

"We're staying at the farm behind the village," explained the girl. "It's nowhere near as cosy as this."

I smiled and went to bring the hot milk for my porridge. She had blonde hair and brown eyes, the very coloring I'd always thought most beautiful in women, the very coloring I'd wanted as a girl, when I'd had to make do with my own gray eyes and coppery mop and be called 'Red Susie' for it. I felt the night on the island had been more of an ordeal for her than for him and that she was actually chilled through, for as soon as she had finished her eggs she took her chair and backed it round toward the stove. I keep the stove on all the time, even in the hottest weather, to dry out the house and the bed-linen and all the sea-dampness I bring in on my feet and clothes. Now this girl sat in front of it staring at the salty blue flames licking round the driftwood burning there. She had tiny fingers with perfectly-formed nails. I suppose like any woman I looked for rings and saw none. So they weren't married. So who cared? I just wondered what stage of their relationship they were at. Had they met at work or College or been the boy and girl next door and known each other since school? They didn't look old enough to have made a habit of anything, and I was pleased for them on that account alone.

"How old is this place?" The man looked up at the wooden ceiling as he spoke.

"The whole thing dates from just after World War Two," I explained, "with some of these interior fittings from the Nineteen-Seventies, I guess. If you're really interested in the house you can look outside and see where I had to knock off the old porch before I could put the verandah on. It was pretty well run down when I got it--and it's a constant job keeping the paintwork right with all the sea winds and salt spray. The front door is just coming up for its re-varnish. Every year it gets a new coat of yacht-varnish. D'you realize there's nothing between my front door and Norway? Lucky I like painting."

"Oh, I'd say you keep it very nicely. This sort of holiday home must be fetching a good price these days. You have one of the best views in England."

"That's true. D'you want to make me an offer?"

"Well, I wouldn't mind living here." He was looking out of the window and across the sea. "I wouldn't mind at all." He had said 'I' not 'we', as if in these sudden hopes and plans the girl would not be included and not matter to him. Perhaps they were not as close as I had imagined; perhaps she was just his casual girl-friend, some little fool who trusted a hard-nosed property speculator.

"I think you'd find it very lonely. I'm not selling, anyhow. This is my bolt-hole from London. I know how lucky I am to have this place."

"We really must go," said the girl, standing up and smoothing her jeans. "They'll be mad with worry at the farm."

"Heavens, yes." The man was suddenly sharing her new

27

agitation. "What'll we tell them?

"The truth," I grinned, opening the front door. Morning sunshine streamed in like a blessing with a fresh smell of the sea. "You went exploring like two kids, got caught on the island, and this weird American lady shipped you off. That *is* the truth, isn't it?"

"More or less," he chuckled, raising his eyebrows at his own embarrassment.

"Okay—my version of the night's events it is."

It would probably sound better at the farm than confessing to a night of screwing on the rocks.

"Did you do this?"

The girl was looking at a watercolor pinned on the inside of the door.

"Yes, I paint."

"Do you paint a lot?" asked the man.

"Some."

"It's very good," he said. "Well, thank you again." He shook my hand. "You've been most hospitable."

"The breakfast was lovely."

The girl's smile was sweet and pretty as she thanked me and again I wondered where these two lived and how their lives went along when they weren't on holiday. There was no reason to think they could be anything special to me, but I had liked them quickly. Quite unexpectedly, I had enjoyed having them in my house.

"Call in again before you go." I waved from the verandah. "Perhaps the circumstances won't be so dramatic next time."

"We might just do that—thanks."

They waved back.

"And look out for the tide!"

They waved again. I watched them for a little while as they hurried along the beach, then I went back inside to wash the dishes. I felt terribly lonely, and wished I had known this place in the early days with Jack. I wished I'd had children, too: children to grow up strong and beautiful, to grow into love like those two, to take part of my soul with them into new lives, and not leave me

alone, here at the edge of the sea,
remembering old things.

2 The Past

Why do I begin to remember old things when new ones should occupy my thoughts? On quiet nights, when the house is in order and I have eaten and put everything away and there isn't a storm to listen to, it seems as if the past is all there is, the present is nothing but the past caught up with today, and a future can't exist.

It was London in the Nineteen-Sixties and the play was *A Midsummer Night's Dream*: a glorious West End production with big stars to play Oberon and Titania and me to design the set. It was the biggest thing ever to happen in my career and I had Jack to thank for it. We had just been married in New York and we were all set for a delayed honeymoon in Rome when Jack finished his current run on Broadway…but then he was offered the part of Professor Higgins in this glossy revival of *Pygmalion* to open in London and tour the provinces.

He told me when we met up for a lunch-break walk in Central Park.

"Hello, Darling," he breathed into my neck. "Made it at last."

"Hiya, Sweetie. I've gotta say it again: this beats any conventional honeymoon."

"Really?" He sounded genuinely delighted. "You know that's marvelous to hear, especially when I remember you were afraid I'd be so terribly conventional." Then he told me about going to London to do *Pygmalion*. I told him I was thrilled. "Thrilled? Seriously? I was rather worried you'd be upset, not going to Rome."

"No, no—Rome can wait. It wasn't built in a day, y'know; why rush there when we can have a fantastic honeymoon in the West End? You playing Higgins, me designing *Dream*...and don't think I've forgotten who I gotta thank for all this." I hugged him hard. "That wonderful moment in your dressing-room when you

32

told your agent you wouldn't play Higgins unless your new and enormously talented wife could be sure of some work in London too. I'm going to remember that all my life."

"Well, that's what agents are for, Darling. Anyway, we'll go to Rome when this work's over."

"Okay, but right now I love the idea of going to London for this job. And I love you. Isn't it just wonderful? At last I got lucky with a famous English actor...after all these years of going out with no-hopers from stage-crews."

"Fame is all tiresome nonsense, Darling. More often than not it's just down to a few good publicity photographs and a decent review in the papers."

"Oh come on, Jack, don't be so 'English' about everything. You have enormous talent."

"I have indeed enormous talent."

"And it's been recognized: you're hugely successful."

"Hugely."

"Stop teasing me!"

"You're the tease. That's one of the reasons I married you."

"Okay--but take stock and be happy. You're the suave English gentleman type; handsome, and just a little weary-looking." I cheekily traced a line down his face. "Perfect as Higgins, and plenty more parts by Bernard Shaw. And all those parts in Noël Coward and Terence Rattigan. What do they call them? 'Plays of Style'? You got style. You're an actor of style. On top of that you could be in every thriller or whodunnit: the well-to-do doctor, the successful businessman, the commanding officer, the master of foxhounds, the captain of industry, the elegant millionaire."

"Yes, but I'm no method actor you know. I have no real technique; it's all intuitive, a gift, I suppose you'd call it. The terrible truth is, Darling, I can only really be myself."

"Well, that's just it! That's your great strength. You only have to transfer your own style of Savile Row suit and Bentley Continental from your own life to to the stage and everyone'll be convinced. They are already. You'll carry *Pygmalion* beautifully. Your Higgins is gonna be a man-about-town, not a dry academic. The public are going to love your raciness and the critics are going to admire your lightness of touch. I'm hugely happy for us both."

"Who needs a good review when one is married to this relentless advertising copywriter-cum-publicity machine?"

"I love you."

And I did love him. There, in Central Park with the noise of New York all around us and London's West End just over our horizon, I loved my witty, handsome, talented husband.

It really had been a great moment when Jack's agent Lydia had called his dressing-room from London. Even while she was speaking we had both decided the trip to Rome could wait and that our real honeymoon would be on the English stage, working together in London for the first time. It seemed like a gift from the gods; gods who were completely on our side. I hugged Jack hard and told him he was the best thing that had ever happened in my life and kissed him under the chin — which was a dangerous thing to do just before a show because it always turned him on and he'd go out there as randy as Hell and forget his lines. He smiled down at me and said I'd better watch out because when we eventually did get to Rome he'd need a honeymoon more than ever and that he'd have no problems playing Higgins because teaching Eliza the King's English would be a piece of cake after dealing with my Yankee squawk. We laughed about that and it was a lovely moment and I had the jet flight to Europe to excite me and everything to look forward to and it was like a new lease of life.

* * *

I loved London in those days and I could never quite contain my joy at making it my new home. It was exciting and mysteriously romantic; very different from the romantic excitement of New York. It was lordly and squalid, strange and familiar, cosy and brash, hectic and peaceful all at the same time. I realize now that London—and all of us—were in the middle of a revolution; but while I was intrigued by the peacock-coloured shirts and ties, the mini-skirts, the pop music and the pirate radio, the psychedelic paint and patchouli-scented boutiques, and realized they marked a new era in British life as surely as the tall glass buildings, it was to the rhythms of an older London that I swung that year.

We lived in Jack's flat, not far from Regent's Park in a once very classy and now highly desirable part of London which was then in a kind of forgotten decline. The rich and aristocratic families had moved out during the War; the developers had yet to move in with their new décor and fancy prices. To be really fashionable we should have lived in Chelsea—but I didn't care. I loved the canal and the zoo and the tree-lined avenues and the sound of my new English shoes as I walked through the lush green parks. I was delighted by the growling black cabs and the dazzling soldiers on parade, by the softly-swishing limousines and the cries of the paper-boys, by the red buses for the town and the green buses for the country, and by the famous streets and buildings I'd learnt about as a child and could now visit whenever I chose. It was an old-fashioned, touristy, innocent response to London: a kind of American fantasy come true; but it really did seem like that to me then, and of course it was embodied in Jack himself. I remember the day I realized this most perfectly. It was when Jack had taken me to Trafalgar Square to be photographed among the pigeons. Of course he was recognized and was charming to the autograph-hunters, of course he was covered in pigeons and had his suit well clawed and pecked, of course he swore at the photographers calling them a bunch of spivs—but I know he loved it really and I knew he was genuinely proud of the Landseer lions and the National Gallery…as proud as I was of my new hat. That same afternoon he took me on a river-cruise to Greenwich. It was just a trip for tourists under the famous bridges and past the Tower, but it taught me more about Jack and more about the English and more about what really stirred my new husband than the months of knowing and loving him in New York. It was a bright, gleaming day on the river. Jack was as happy as a child to have me in his arms with his beloved history sliding past us on either bank. He outdid the boatman's commentary with his tales of Queen Elizabeth the First and of Shakespeare's Globe, of the Crown Jewels and St. Paul's, of the Great Fire and Sir Christopher Wren, and of the statues of the Queen's Beasts standing guard at Hampton Court far upstream the other way where we'd go tomorrow. I was under his quiet spell of romance, under the spell of a proud Shakespearian England whose echoes still came to us today: an England I would re-create on stage in this very city. As we re-embarked at Greenwich a fresh breeze blew up the river, sparkling tiny diamonds on the Thames wavelets, bringing sea-smells into London from the wide flat coast and the cold Northern waters whose moods I had yet to learn...the sea beyond my window, waking me up with its blue light and gull-cries.

3 The Door

The warm days continued with plenty of sunshine, but a less perfect sky: the pure blue became shot over with a thin veil of cloud and a sour, alkaline haze came up from the South. When you live by the sea you are sensitive to these tiny changes, while casual visitors to the beach might scarcely notice any difference. Jennie was out every morning, walking the horses one way and cantering them back the other. By mid-day the sky was clearing again to a fresher blue with brighter clouds; a few families had appeared with picnics and children were paddling off the warm, smooth sand.

I decided this was the windless day to re-paint my front door. It's a job I do every year. The door faces due East across the sea and, if neglected, the salt and sun and wind and rain soon scour it to the texture of that bleached driftwood which so often litters the beach, smashed and sea-rubbed to twigs or reared up in sticks and branches like the bare bones of a dinosaur. I had taken the door off its hinges and had it supported on chairs for a good sandpapering. The sun came warmly to the smooth wood, drying it perfectly. Now I was laying on the clean-smelling yacht-varnish...and listening to a cassette on my portable player.

Music has always been a big part of my life. That's why I bring a stack of cassettes to the house and play a different one each day: carefully, never wastefully, so I can renew my pleasure in the music as if I were hearing it for the first time yet knowing it is already in my soul. When I'm living in town my favourites are Count Basie, Django Reinhardt, Stephane Grapelli, Gershwin and Cole Porter; but when I live beside the sea I go for the older masters like Mozart, Tchaikovsky and Mahler, and for Rachmaninov, who seems to inhabit the best of both worlds. Sure, it can be melancholy, but it's always rich and wonderful too. If you go back far enough in my family you'll find some Hungarian ancestors, so I guess that old romantic Europe is still in my spirit. The music I love never fails to bring it out.

To accompany this varnishing job I had chosen the ravishing *Four Last Songs* by Richard Strauss. It was a cassette I rarely played. I had almost forgotten how emotional the music was and I became quite lost in the mixture of its soaring phrases and my long strokes of varnish beneath the warm sky. It was in a kind of dream that I saw figures approaching through the dunes and recognized the two people I had rescued from the island. They waved a cheerful greeting. When they came up to me we began talking as if we had been parted for less than an hour. I didn't want to be rude, but I kept the conversation short: my eyes on the varnish, my ears on the music. I can never talk over music and must always listen with the whole of my being—but they persisted in chatting to me. They had been for long walks and had come to know the coastline better. We spoke briefly about the weather and the horses on the beach.

"Anyway," said the girl, "we thought you should have this."

She presented what was obviously a bottle of wine wrapped in tissue paper.

"Thank you," I replied, genuinely pleased by their gesture. "Thank you very much."

"After all," the man was saying, "you did save our lives."

"Now that has to be an exaggeration," I chuckled. "Maybe I saved you from getting wet — or getting pneumonia. But it's very kind of you anyhow." I pulled off the paper. "It's white!" I exclaimed.

"I hope you like white wine," said the man.

"Oh I do...only you look like the kind of people who'd drink red."

"You look like the sort of person who'd drink white," he replied, smiling handsomely.

"You're right," I admitted. "Why do we think these things? I don't know. But I know I like this bottle."

Suddenly I wanted to smile and laugh like this for ever, warm and easy outside my house with the sun above me and his eyes upon me. I wanted them to stay and drink the wine with me but they said they had to be going.

"I like your music," said the man.

I kept working but said: "Me too."

"It's wonderful," said the girl.

"Strauss's *Four Last Songs*," I explained, laying down another stroke of varnish, trying to finish the whole door before any of it dried.

"You work to music," continued the man. "That's wonderful, too."

"I hope it'll be smooth," I smiled.

"It will be," he said. "The music is getting into the varnish."

"Yes," I mused. "Yes. That's rather wonderful too, isn't it?"

It *was* a wonderful thought. A kind of sword went through me. I pretended to look for brush-hairs.

"Here," said the man. "I'll lift one end for you. It's all right, I'll keep my fingers off the wet bits."

He raised up the door to the horns of Richard Strauss and the whole sky was suddenly reflected in my varnish. He had brought its magnificent blue down here to me; now, like a tender god playing with new power, he was raising its lake between us: a lake of every color and every passion known to man, to woman, to god and goddess. My glittering, sun-spangled reflection swung down before me and was again swallowed in the lake of light: blue, blue, impossibly, gloriously blue. And the music was raised up, too: sweet Autumnal music composed at the end of an artist's life, raised up with the soprano into the freshness of a new Spring. Years of loss and loneliness had gone to the fire in the hot blue light; now the glory was renewed with an innocent and rapturous delight in color, smell and sound—opening my soul to the blue of the sky and the sea below it, the sparkle of light across the door, the sun across his face. He rested the door down again and I made a great show of peering into the paintwork, but my heart was bursting with joy and my whole body stirring with new wonders. As I bent forward, a fringe of hair fell across my eyes. I felt his fingers stroke it gently aside. That was when I knew he loved me — even as I stood there pretending to look for imperfections in the varnish, even as the girl stood near us, fresher, younger and prettier than I could ever be. That was when I knew he loved me — and when I loved him for loving me, and for knowing it.

4 The Set

I had never designed Shakespeare before. From a purely professional point of view I felt honored to have been given the chance, not awed or worried as some of my friends said I should have been. And to get a *Midsummer Night's Dream* was the icing on the cake. It had always been one of my favorite plays and I was determined to make the most of this marvelous opportunity. I wanted to do something quitessentially English, something to honor Shakespeare and the English stage and to celebrate my own arrival here with Jack. Was that dangerously old-fashioned and self-indulgent? Was it corny and pompous? I didn't think so; didn't think some people might laugh at me. For I had always believed that every public artistic venture needed a personal vision to drive it—and I would say so to anyone who needed convincing I had taken this bull by the horns.

My idea was to set the play in an English garden, for although

Shakespeare gives the scene as 'Athens and a wood near it', *A Midsummer Night's Dream* had always struck me as one of the most English of his plays: his ancient Greeks had purely English manners and attitudes; only the supernatural characters seemed foreign and 'other-worldly'. That too had to be stongly suggested in the design: a tension between the innocent and the sensual, the ordered and the wild. Shakespeare's nostalgia for an England even merrier than his own would be carried by the rustic innocence of Bottom and his friends. The struggles between Oberon and Titania and Puck's bewitching of the mortals would symbolize the darker and more elemental forces of both the natural and supernatural worlds: the powers that fired the lusts of men and women and that spun the globe. So the English garden set would need to be 'flown' to reveal another: the wood — a dreamlike perversion of the garden, paradise with a touch of nightmare, full of strangely-shaped trees, trails of colourful flowers, outsized blooms, a riot of vegetation, gigantic fungi, and deep shadows.

Getting these ideas was the easy bit. When I said all this at one of our first production meetings I found myself ploughing through humps and troughs of arguments I'd never even thought of. Simply because I had come from New York and was known for work on some dance shows, the producers expected a kind of female Busby Berkeley. Where was the urban glamour, the showbiz, the schmaltz? Why couldn't the set look like *West Side Story*? When I made it clear I wasn't doing Broadway, somebody suggested I should do Hollywood: design the whole thing to look like a film-studio with a movie of Shakespeare's play in production and the audience as extras. I wasn't sure who was joking and who was serious and how much of a disappointment I was already.

Then there was the Director, who didn't agree with anybody. He was a young modernist of the most vehement variety who would have liked to stir up the West End with a bare-stage production and everyone in jeans. He knew he'd never get away with that, but he still thought I'd gone too far the other way with my lush and complex designs, my taste for nostalgia, my interest in subtlety and attention to detail. He, more than any of them, really infuriated me—for it was he who wanted to take away the wonder and magic of the play, to reduce it to a set of angry exchanges, to deflower my dream, and with it the dreams of the audience and of Shakespeare himself. There were moments in that meeting when I was ready to pack up, say 'no thanks', forget the whole thing and wait for Jack to take me out of it to Rome—but when the Director started arguing with me and his long face became animated with his own crude ideas for design and he ran his bony fingers through his close-cropped hair, making jokes with the actors to get them on his side, I knew I'd ride this out more firmly than any storm I'd faced before. I would get my way with him and with all of them. I would go above everyone's head if I had to; yell to the cast, the crew, the press, the producers and the backers. This would be the best, the lushest, most dramatic, beautiful, fantastic and glorious design in London and everyone would see I'd been right. I'd fill the theater, get the best reviews and make money — without sacrificing one principle of Shakespeare, Art, or Truth. With a smile of glittering charm — a quality for which I obviously wasn't going to be remembered on this show — I put my drawings back into their folder.

"I'm so sorry, everyone," I said. "We're sticking with these. Come to think of it, " I added with an even broader smile, "I'm not sorry at all. Your bosses are paying me plenty; I'd like to make sure they get their money back."

* * *

Jack had already opened in *Pygmalion* and the night after that meeting we walked back together out of Leicester Square into the darker, quieter streets. It was the early hours, everyone had gone home, London felt like our own. Jack was getting terrific notices and they had put him in bullish mood.

"So, you upset the brown-jumpered sod, eh?"

I hugged his arm.

"*You* don't need to be nasty to my Director, Darling. That's going to be *my* job. He's not all bad, either."

"But he is. He's got no more talent than my arse, and his career's pointing the same way, if you ask me. Truth is, my arse is more talented…and it'll definitely be better-looking, as you should jolly well know."

Jack had been drinking.

"Oh Jack," I was quite secure in my decision to go my own way, "you needn't be horrible like that. Gavin's only doing his best."

"But his best isn't bloody good enough, is it? He's one of the bare-board brigade; should be up North in some sordid kitchen-sink stuff with his angry young friends, all part of life's threadbare tapestry. Look!" Jack suddenly pointed up at a café sign. "Look at that. That's him. Bloody *Late Nite Snax* spelled the wrong bloody way. God, how I hate that! That's him all over, bastardizing the English language. Old Willie'll be spinning in his grave to think someone like that's got his hands on *Dream*; thank God Lydia and I put you on the job as well. It'll only get worse, you know; in ten year's time…less…we'll be getting signs like that all over the place: *Fish 'n' Chips, Beer 'n' Byte*—they'll go the whole bloody hog. And it'll be his fault, him and his cheapskate beatnik buggers, stumbling from crisis to crisis and calling it a career…"

"That's unfair, Jack." Our heels rang through the empty night. "I don't like Gavin as a man and I don't much like his design ideas either, but I have to admit he's got a feel for language. He knows the script inside out; he does care about the text."

"Well, that's just it, isn't it?

He should be talking it through with scruffy students in some concrete nightmare of a college, not putting on a show in the West End. I tell you, you could be doing the last decent *Dream* for a decade."

Jack went on, cursing into the black air, and I walked with his arm in mine, keeping my temper down and my sorrow at bay. I understood Jack. Certainly, I revolted against the easy way out, the stock-in-trade solution, the whim of fashion, the cliché, the dull compromise; that's what had brought me into conflict with Gavin and the others. I'd stick my neck out, because that was the only way to do it, and the day I drew my neck in would be the day I'd be no good. But sticking my neck out didn't mean being rude or crude or bigoted or not listening to the experts or learning from new people—and Jack had forgotten that. He had forgotten that I could cope with my own decisions; he had forgotten his own triumphs in *Pygmalion*. He had forgotten everything but a rage in his head that had begun by his agreeing with me hours ago. The rage was fuelled by alcohol; he had forgotten that he had forgotten. I kissed him, smelling the whisky-warmth of his face and the soap and the trace of missed make-up on his neck.

"Darling, tonight you're a big success. Enjoy it. Don't spoil it by ranting about my little problems."

"But they're not little problems. They're huge bloody world-wide problems and you're stuck in a little microscop...a microcos...a microcosm of them, that's what it is."

Why did Jack have to be drunk tonight; this warm, sweet, English night when he was darling of the West End and I was about to create the best stage-set in London? Why did he have to be drunk when I loved him more than he was capable of knowing; loved him with words and kisses and touches he would so quickly forget?

5 The Beach

Now what was to be done? What *could* be done? I was in love with a man I guessed must be more than twenty years younger than myself. Yes, through that chance meeting and these weird co-incidences, it was true. I recognized the signs well enough: the wonderful lightness of my spirit, the new sparky sense of being, the frantically charged atmosphere of the world around me, joyous amazement that such thrilling changes could take place in my body at the very thought of him. Then there was the simple human happiness I hadn't known for years—too many years, years which had made me an older woman, too old for this young man. Ridiculously, I thought of what my friends from New York and London would have said: 'Heard about old Susie cradle-snatching on the beach?' Jack would have laughed it off, or told me to get on with my final fling and think myself damn lucky that a young man was showing any interest at all. My mother, if she had still been alive, would have simply denounced it as unhealthy in her firm New England manner and tut-tutted me back to the cool and unfussy straight-and-narrow way which had never allowed such complications a foothold in her own life. Maybe she and her kind were lucky...but if I examined my feelings as I lay awake in the sea-hissing night, or put my toes on the warm verandah where morning mist beaded on the new and fragrant varnish of my door, I knew I didn't want this to stop. It was complicated, but it was great! I didn't feel unhealthy and I didn't feel guilty. I felt wonderful. I just wanted to see him again and go on seeing him; to have these marvels in my body again and to go on having them.

So now the bay became an amphitheater of desire and my wooden house its focal point: the place where he had first touched me. From its deliciously varnished door I ran along the beach while sweet winds blew upon me, clear sunlight burned me and green sea-light flooded all around with white birds flashing under the vast blue dome. I stood upon smooth black rocks and looked down into pulsating pools, searching for the shell or sea-anemone that could contain the curl and whip of my longing. I rowed my tiny boat around the island where I had first seen him; stood on its seaweed-covered margin letting cold water suck and swill at my legs; rolled on the tender stripe of grass at its secret middle; opened my shirt to the cool sea wind and put my bare body on the ground for him — for a man whose name I didn't even know. Beneath a Twentieth-Century sky, pale and open, I felt myself consumed by a timeless flame, dark and hot: a woman of the ancient sea-worlds and of this one, transcending my own life to become a creature of complete desire. I played my music and it ran through me like a joyful madness. Naked on my bed or pressed against my wooden walls, my cabin-house afloat on a star-filled night, I stroked my wasted breasts and felt them tingle like a girl's for him. I rubbed my thighs and drew new sweat from my skin. I imagined taking him warm and wet into myself a thousand times. In the morning I would wake, solitary and chill, and see myself as an ageing, lonely, foolish woman. But when the sun rose and the birds cried and the sea rolled and the white waves flew, it would all begin again and I knew I loved him and wanted him and wouldn't say no to his wildest demand.

* * *

But it was the girl I met next, in the village post-office with Jennie. I wanted some milk; she was looking at postcards; Jennie was buying a tin of black mints for the horses.

"Hello!" We all spoke together: three very different women brought together by chance in this little shop warmed by sunshine. But a coldness stabbed into me. This girl was my rival—more than that, my potential enemy—likely to be hot and jealous, ready to hate me for what I most wanted to do. Jennie introduced her as Elaine.

"We've already met," I smiled.

"Under the most ridiculous circumstances," added the girl with a half-embarrassed laugh. "We got stuck on the island and this lady ferried us off."

I didn't like the image of a 'ferry lady'; I saw a storybook character, fat, with black boots and calloused hands. She didn't mean it that way, of course, but I couldn't keep the bristle out of my voice.

"It was nothing at all," I lied.

"Thanks again for the nice breakfast," she giggled.

"No problem."

I juggled my cartons of milk and my money and listened to the girls talking. It was evident that Elaine shared Jennie's passion for horses and that they were arranging a ride from the stables. I studied them: of similar height and build, but Jennie the stronger and bonier in cords and boots with her cascade of curls tossing a red and healthy glow into the shadowed shop.

"Tomorrow morning then," Jennie was saying as she paid for the mints. "The stables are just at the other end of the village, at the big house. They've got a couple of racehorses and a few hacks and a big brute of a hunter—and my favorite, old Julius. Why not come along now and give him a mint? He's very gentle."

Elaine's hair was straight and blonde and a pale, fresh light came from her slender figure in holiday clothes. I felt nothing but envy.

"See ya, Susie!" Jennie mimicked my accent and breezed out of the shop.

"Bye-bye," said Elaine, following her into the brilliant sunshine. I hated myself for being older and less beautiful.

* * *

The next morning I saw the beach was strewn with seaweed

and that a low tide had exposed more rocks than usual. It must have blown up rough during the night, although nothing had woken me, and all was calm enough now. Morning sunshine was already sucking up a rich seaweed smell. I watched the little wading birds scuttle up and down the beach, busily probing the shoreline, while clouds of sand-flies could be better imagined than seen above the heaps of wrack. I decided not to go for my usual walk but to make myself a leisurely breakfast and do some drawing.

I sat on the verandah with my drawing-board and pencils, but I didn't get much work done. As the sun grew hotter and the first few walkers appeared on the beach, I could not help but think of the man whose face and body and movements and dark, magical presence were forever before me. Over and over again I relived the wonderful moments with the varnished door; it was just to one side of me and the sunshine still drew from it a faint and lovely fragrance. Everyone dreams, I thought. When those who dream by night wake up, they lose their dreams into the rush of life; but those who dream by day might mould their dreams to mingle with reality and find new power in their lives—or so it seemed to me as I sat there in the morning sunshine. So I imagined the varnish on the door to contain a layer of his spirit, and that my uncertain and striated reflection in it was a way of being wrapped in his arms. I made the dream and held it, there in the bright morning with the memory of the music and the varnish and the darkness of the shadows across his face and the swishing of the sea. Then horses came along the beach and I went for my binoculars.

Jennie was on Julius, the old gray. Elaine—unfamiliar in a riding-hat—was beside her on a slimmer, dark brown horse. She seemed to ride as well as Jennie, with the same upright seat and easy, firm control. The man was not with them. I guessed he must have stayed behind at the stables.

I wished instantly that I could be with him while Elaine was out with Jennie. Both girls' hair shone in the sun; I could see them talking while the horses nodded their great heads and little wisps of sand spurted from their hooves at the trot. The man was not with them! I thought of rushing through the dunes to steal a moment with him at the stables, the shop, or wherever he might be found. The horses slowed to a walk. Jennie was pointing along the beach. They would soon be passing below the house: the place where Jennie would always wave if she saw me. Elaine, of course, would also wave, for she too would now know where to look. They were probably talking about me right now...but the man was not with them! Where was he, what was he doing, where might I find him? It seemed hopeless. Everything was hopeless. I went inside and closed the door.

6 The Music

Richard the sound engineer was a thin young man with a finely-chiselled profile and pale blue eyes and he managed to look serious even when he was smiling. He usually appeared in a black roll-neck sweater which made him look like a cross between a modern poet and a secret agent and he was not unaware, I think, of the dramatic effect it gave beneath his mop of blond hair, worn fashionably thick and long. As I walked through London to an early appointment with him I hoped for no more trouble. Things had settled down between Gavin and myself and the set and costumes were coming along fine, but I knew my ideas for the sound were crucial to the atmosphere of the whole production, knew they were not strictly my department, and hoped that Richard would see what I meant and be able to do what I asked without any aggravation.

When I got into the theater

the house-lights were up and music was playing: lush, romantic, Nineteenth-Century music I didn't know but which I loved at once. It caught me up in its passionate orchestral sweep as I walked on stage and looked around the auditorium for Richard. The place was vast and empty but convoluted and sinister like the innards of a monster—and I couldn't find him anywhere.

"Hi Richard! Richard?" The music was loud and soft and sweet and sad and my voice didn't go with it but I had to find him. "Richard?" My shoes thumped hard and modern on the stage and I'd have liked to take them off and curl up in one of those red plush seats down there and close my eyes and dream to the music of silk dresses and dark wooden rooms and the flicker of candles—but I had to find him. "Richard? It's Susie. Hell—you gotta be here somewhere!"

"Good morning!"

I nearly jumped out of my skin. His voice thundered round me like the crack of Doom. When I recovered I cast my eyes furiously up and down and round the theater...and the music continued under his disembodied voice.

"Hello there." Now the voice had a chuckle in it. "Nice to see you."

"My God I'd like to see *you*, boy!" I yelled, glancing madly up into the circle and the boxes and into the dusty gantries in the darkness above the stage. "Okay, where are you? Come out. D'you know you scared me white?"

"I'm terribly sorry." His beautifully modulated voice, still unseen, came richly from the hidden loudspeakers and the music stopped. "I'm up in the lighting box. I was just trying something out. I'll be down straight away."

"No, no—don't stop the music," I shouted into the roof. "the music's great. Just don't scare me, okay?" But the music didn't start again and Richard appeared as if by magic beside me, apologetic without being embarrassed.

"I'm terribly sorry," he told

me again. "Was my voice very loud on the speakers?"

"Boy, I'll say it was!"

"I *am* sorry. I'll get you a coffee."

"Thanks." We walked backstage towards his room. "The music was lovely though. I liked the music. What was it?"

He gave me a serious look that seemed to ask: 'How did you get to your age and not know that music?'

"Wagner's *Siegfried Idyll*."

"Oh, Wagner. It's terrific."

"It's beautiful; one of the most perfect pieces he ever wrote. D'you know why he wrote it?" Richard had forgiven my ignorance and was looking forward to telling a story. But I hadn't expected him to be this voluble so early in the morning, perhaps unfairly hadn't expected the serious young man in the black sweater to be enthusiastic about anything beyond his perplexing sound equipment. "Wagner wrote it as a Birthday present for his wife. He had it played for her in their house, when she came down to dinner, I think. Imagine the scene..." Richard was leading me through the brick-lined passages to his room and I thought: 'he's telling me all this as if he's known me for years and he really cares about it and it's going to make everything we do together sweet and easy.'

"...It's 1870, in Wagner's villa on Lake Luzern. Wagner's written the *Idyll*, refined it 'til it's perfect, scored it for a small orchestra he can get into the house; now he smuggles them in while his wife's upstairs, then has them play just as she's coming out of the bedroom. Quite a Birthday present, eh?"

It was. It sent a glow through me.

"He must have loved her very much," I said.

"Oh, he did."

"Well, it's fine music. I must listen to it properly."

"Yes indeed. Here we are then."

Once more he was the cool young man in black surrounded by his machines and mugs of milky coffee. I saw him once again as a natural inhabitant of the brash new London with its tall glass buildings, brutal concrete pillars and cold steel stairways—but despite his chilly professionalism I had seen into his heart with that music and I knew we had a better chance of some honest and shared understanding in our work.

"So I need three things, Richard." I drank his coffee and told him my ideas. "I need music for Theseus's garden: that's every scene that's not in the wood, but a different piece each time, okay? I need music for the wood itself—less formal, more dreamy—and I need some birdsong or cricket sounds for the wood as well; but I want something done to the sound so it's like a dream, so it's mysterious and unreal, so that every time there's a transition into the wood the audience know they're in the supernatural. And I want you to use sound in a way it's probably never been used here before—as part of the design, so that people are completely wrapped up in it by the way it sounds, just as they are drawn into the set by the way it looks. D'you get it? D'you see what I mean? Can you help me?" I saw him looking at my mouth. I still wore bright red lipstick and lacquered my nails to match. No doubt his girl-friends would wear the new silvery pinks with their pale frosted lips. Well, if he thought I was old-fashioned — tough.

"It's a marvelous idea," he smiled, "a whole series of marvelous ideas. I know just how to do it..." And he went through the most wonderful sound-plot I had ever heard. He would record stately Elizabethan lute music for the scenes with Theseus and an especially melancholy fall of notes for transitions to the wood: one of Dowland's courtly dances, slowed down and played through an echo-chamber. Then he would take recordings of a night in a jungle and slow those down, too, mixing sweet English blackbirds and nightingales in tantalizing counterpoint. And he would have new loudspeakers rigged around the auditorium to surround everyone with the music and the sounds so that they would not be perceived as coming off the stage but be part of the imagination. He knew a lot about Elizabethan music and assured me, in the words of an old poem, that his choice would 'ravysshe humayne sense'. "Pop in whenever you like," he added with a smile, "and hear how it's coming along. There's always plenty of coffee in my room. By the way," he shook my hand in farewell, "I've seen your drawings: superb. I love the set—and don't forget, you can borrow my Wagner record when I've finished dubbing it."

* * *

Not everyone was as obliging as Richard, but his intuitive understanding of what I wanted and his unlikely but genuine friendship gave me great confidence...and I needed all I could get when Kaplin the impresario had me in his office. It was high above London in one of the new tower-blocks: a simple, square room with an uncomfortably low ceiling but stunning, slap-in-the-face views from two sides of window. Kaplin stood up: thin, balding, expensively dressed, full of worried energy. I had always got on well with theater bosses and producers. Those who were suspicious of artists could be won over by my reputation for hard work and sledgehammer common sense; the stuffy, distant ones I wooed with what other people told me was a natural charm. Yet I felt there was trouble brewing here. This was the man who had signed my contract and by whose whim I was working in a West End show, but at the launch party I hadn't warmed to him at all. He had a faintly middle-European Jewish voice and manner which should have endeared him to me — my old family had come from the same roots — but I never saw him smile once and I sensed he would be cold and difficult. Now I was in his office I saw it had no atmosphere of showbusiness: no photographs of stars, no flowers, no awards, not even a flashy pen. It was all business and no show. The most dramatic thing was the view — but of course he wasn't going to give me time to look at that.

"Good morning, Miss Conrad." Despite my being married to Jack, Kaplin persisted in using what he would think of as my stage-name. I wasn't going to be impressed. "And how are we getting on?" He knew damn well how I was getting on.

"The set's going in next week," I told him blankly.

"Ah yes, the set. You know, Miss Conrad," he sat down and waved me to a chair, "not everyone is perfectly happy about the set. It's proving to be rather expensive — we don't necessarily mind that — but it's, well, not quite what we expected. You see, your last shows on Broadway were very exciting, very exciting indeed. We greatly admired that musical you did: very vibrant, very daring; and that up-dated *Saint Joan* with the space-ship and the angels: new, brilliant, outrageous. We all loved that. But

Gavin tells me this is rather old-fashioned."

"It's an old-fashioned play, Mister Kaplin," I smiled brilliantly, "written over three-hundred years ago, you know. Isn't that something?"

Kaplin didn't acknowledge the joke or admit the insult. He spread his hands and tried to look as if he could plead and dictate at the same time.

"Relevance, Miss Conrad. Relevance!"

"I guess it's as relevant now as it ever was; no more and no less."

I had succeeded in exasperating him and provoked a classic one-liner.

"This *is* the Nineteen-Sixties."

I saw red and stood up.

"So it is, Mister Kaplin, so it is. But I'm not going to turn *A Midsummer Night's Dream* into *Shakespeare Swings to London Town* just to fall in with some flash-in-the-pan fashion. It's a great play and I've designed a great set and the public are going to love it because they know a good show when they see one...and if you don't, you can fire me now."

He waved me back down into my seat.

"Really, Miss Conrad. Don't be so rash, so hasty. Take care."

"I do take care!" I blazed on. "I take care right enough. I take care with everything I do and I always have. I love this business and I love this play and if I didn't I wouldn't be arguing with you now."

"No. Quite." He was very dry. "Is it your habit to argue with everyone on a production?"

"Only if I have to — and by God I've had to on this one." I got to my feet again. "Your people here have fought me every inch of the way and I can't see why. What's the matter with you all? Okay, what's the matter with *me*? I'm too honest, aren't I? I care too much about my work. It's not just a job to pass the time, make a bit of money and meet supposedly interesting people. It's art, it's entertainment, it's magic, it's people's dreams, it matters for itself! I'm not here to have some kinda fun holiday in your West End, I'm here to do the best damn job I can, and if you want a second-rate one, you can hire any old shomoken from local rep and give him the only break of his life. You say you liked my Broadway shows — well this one beats 'em hollow for style and subtlety. It's better work; it's the best thing I've done, I know it, and I'm not ashamed to say so. You think the set's old-fashioned, but have you seen how it transforms into that fantastic jungle I've made for you? Have you heard about the sound-effects? I've got the latest technology working for you there. That young guy Richard, he's gonna make the sound like nothing else in London, like nothng else anywhere. And the lighting..."

"Ah yes," he interrupted with infuriating calm, "the lighting. Our lighting director says it's impossible."

"That's because he's lighting some damn set of his own, not mine! It's either full of shadows or it's washed out. I've tried to make him see what I need. That garden in the opening scene: it's Merrie England, it's warm, it's golden, it's the sweet pure light of an English paradise: the England that never was but that everybody longs for. It has to look warm and honeyed like a glade in Vermont. Have you ever seen a glade in Vermont, Mister Kaplin? Have you ever dreamed you were Robin Hood in Sherwood Forest before the world grew old and dirty? Did you ever take a girl on a hayride on a September afternoon when the sky was bluer and the sun was warmer and the girls were prettier? Have you ever been in one of those rose-gardens at a house where Queen Elizabeth stayed? Have you ever driven through Oxfordshire in a sports car on the first day of Spring? Have you ever looked out of a castle window and seen the cornfields stretching away across England and wanted to cry? Have you? Well it doesn't matter if you haven't, because as soon as I get that set lit right, that's what you're gonna be feeling and that's what the audiences are gonna be feeling. And tell me this, Mister Kaplin:

have you ever had a nightmare, one of those dreams where everything's too big or the wrong shape and you don't know what's round the next corner or behind you and you can't keep your balance and you feel like you're in someone's power? Well, that's the feeling you'll get when you're in the enchanted wood and Puck's ready to put the magic dust on your eyes...so long as it ain't lit up like Brooklyn Bridge! Now if that's old-fashioned I'm glad I'm old-fashioned, and if that upsets Gavin he sure needs upsetting. Am I running away with your budget? Am I frighteneing audiences away? Am I making you look stupid in front of the critics? No! I'm doing my job making dreams come true the best way I know how — and if you don't want that job done I'll stop doing it now!"

I was red and hectic and sat back sweating in my chair. Kaplin looked as if a bomb had gone off in his belly. He adjusted his tie and his sleeves and the remains of his hair.

"Yes, well, er, we — I mean I — I don't want you to stop, Miss Conrad. I don't want you to stop at all. I just wanted a chat, just a chat about how we might all make things a little easier on this production."

"You know how you can do that," I fired right back at him. "You can do that by keeping all these no-talent jerks off my back."

"Indeed. Well, I really think that's all for now."

"I hope so. I truly hope so."

Poor Mister Kaplin. I'd been really tough on him and he'd kept his temper like a true Britisher. I wasn't making it any easier for him now the crisis was over—but I hadn't taken my career this far by apologizing for my work and I wasn't starting now.

"Right." He made it clear that the audience really was at an end. "I'll drop in and watch a rehearsal or two. By the way, I hear Jack is doing very nicely in *Pygmalion*. I must confess I haven't seen it yet but I'll be going as soon as I can. The reviews are most gratifying, aren't they? Everyone says it's a great success. I'm so pleased for you both."

He was smiling, showing me

out, and I felt terrible. I thought I really had gone too far and been rude and damaged everything I'd been trying to preserve and now here he was being so damn *nice* to me. But no, I steeled myself, it was just that snobby old humbling technique the British were so good at. If I said I was sorry now, I'd lose whatever respect I might have gained. I would just have to leave him thinking I was a loud bitch...but as long as he thought I was a loud bitch who cared passionately about her work, I wouldn't mind.

"Please try to see eye-to-eye with Gavin." Kaplin extended his last trick with an urbanely manicured hand. "I think he will be a great director one day. If that day hasn't yet come, let's all bear with him. Well, I'm sure I'll see you soon. Goodbye."

"Goodbye, Mister Kaplin."

I went out feeling two feet tall.

I spent too much money on a new hat, had lunch with Jack, and told him everything.

"Dear me," he scowled. "I'm

afraid you've sailed close to the wind with Kaplin. I suppose I'll have to sweeten him for you and put it all right."

"Don't do that, please. I'll fight my own battles. He was in high dudgeon and all set to give me a lecture—but I gave *him* one instead."

"So it seems. From what you've told me, it sounds like you were the one in 'high dudgeon'."

"No, I didn't set out to ruin his day at all, but I wasn't going to be told how to do my job either. The worst thing was, he tried to be charming at the end of it."

"Well," Jack continued to look uncomfortable, "I know Kaplin's an unctious old bugger, but he is one of the most influential men in London, definitely top dog. I really think you should apologise to him."

"I will not!"

"But you'll have to, Sue. I know you see your life as some kind of saga, and all the people who come into contact with you as representations of the epic forces you see in everything—but Kaplin doesn't see it that way. Why should he? All he cares about is making money..." Jack folded his napkin and waved his fingers at the waiter "...and if *he* doesn't make money, none of *us* do either."

"I know that, Jack, but I've got allies in this. All the cast love my ideas and Richard knows exactly what I want."

"Richard? Who's Richard? Er—yes, another brandy please, and this napkin is dirty. Richard who?"

"Richard Bennett, the sound man."

"The sound man? The bloody sound man? D'you think Kaplin will listen to him? He won't even know who he is. For God's sake grow up, Sue. Kaplin doesn't give a monkey's toss about the sound man—and he only gives one about you because he's paying you so much and Lydia told him to. Look, you'll have to go back to him and tell him you're sorry. You'll get away with it because you're an American and because he knows me, but you'll have to say something. Doesn't matter what it is; you don't even have to mean it. I'm confident you'll sink to the occasion. Even though he's a queer I imagine Kaplin is also a ladies' man. Why not show him your tits at the same time? Might do some good."

I put down my fork and stared at Jack.

"I can't believe this," I said. "I can't believe you can be so...so vile! You're as bad as Kaplin; worse, you're dishonest and coarse, like most men. If Kaplin was a woman I'd fix him straight off."

"Kaplin as a woman, eh? Now there's a thought. He'd make a bloody peculiar woman." Jack contemplated his brandy. "Does that mean you'd sleep with him to get what you want...I mean sleep with 'her'?"

"Why d'you have to be so disgusting? Why can't you just support me in this?"

"It's not a question of supporting you, Darling, it's a question of common sense. If you don't put it right with old Kaplin you'll never work here again. Come to think of it, neither will I. Now we can't have that, can we? Don't worry, I'll sort something out. You see it's all a question of compromise."

"You say that to me when *I'm* the one trying to bring some stability to this show?"

"Stability? You're about as stable as an Italian government."

"Oh am I? Am I indeed?" The restaurant chatter died around us. "It's only what you call compromise because people haven't got the guts to stick out for their own ideas!"

"Sue, for God's sake, it's the Café Royal."

"I don't care if it's your Buckingham Palace. I'm not having this show run into the ground by some moneychanger who can't tell *A Midsummer Night's Dream* from a wet dream in Soho!" Jack's mouth was slightly open. "And if we never work for him again then we'll be lucky!" A waiter appeared—and disappeared. "I'll show them. I'll show them all. And if I have to show you, I'll show *you* too!" I snatched up my gloves and bawled at him. "Break a leg tonight and have an extra brandy for me!"

I stormed out, only to be tweaked at the door by an old lady.

"I say," she shrilled, laden with furs and as deaf as a post, "isn't that our celebrated Professor Higgins you're lunchin' with? I confess I wish I were a gel again, bein' escorted by him. An ector of great charm, and so well suited to the part, I feel. Good day to you."

I was in the street, hot, with my feet stamping along and my face wet. Why were they all doing this to me? Why would they put my dream in the dust? Why was Jack being so difficult, so damn British? Was all of Europe like this: petty and pathetic, crooked and impossible? In no time at all I found myself back at the theater where a long morning's rehearsal was just finishing.

"Hi Susie! Hello there!" The actors were coming out, vital and hungry, the actresses tidying their hair. "*Love* your coat, Susie." The crew were sweeping up. "Nice hat, luv. Been to see the Queen, 'ave yer?"

I brushed past them all, head

down, hurrying to find a quiet seat at the back of the stalls where I could fold up and calm down and sort myself out. There, in the dim auditorium, I sobbed hot, angry, frustrated tears. But then there was music: soft, warm, tender music drifting round me. I dried my eyes and looked up, sniffing horribly. On the stage was Emma Harrison — the little blonde who played Hermia — obviously stopped in her tracks on her way out; at the same time I recognized the music as Wagner's *Siegfried Idyll*. Emma took off her beret and looked around like a grown up Alice in Wonderland enraptured by the music. I slunk lower in my seat, not wishing to be seen by her or anyone. The music I had first heard with Richard swelled and rolled and soared around the empty theater and the faint noise of traffic outside was lost and the whole world seemed to be filled by the wondering girl on the stage in her everyday clothes with the music so sad, so happy, so pure. Beyond this theater, all England might run to the cold seas, all the sunshine sun and Summer might roll about us, but the whole world was supended here on the rise and fall of music. I saw Richard come out from the wings and take Emma in his arms. I saw them kiss and laugh and stroke each other's hair. I saw him take from his jacket pocket a brightly wrapped present which she opened. It was a necklace, gleaming even under the bland house lights. He put it on her and kissed her again on the neck and the lips and I understood it all perfectly. And that was when I cried my bitterest tears and realized that Jack would never do anything like this for me. In the darkness of the theater I said to myself: 'Love is all that matters and everything else stinks and I vow that one day I'll make pure love count for more than anything I'm going through right now.' Then I buried my face in my hands and wept aloud and felt a pain through my body and could no longer hear the music properly or see them walk out for her Birthday party.

7 The Talk

I saw him beyond the window. He came through the dunes, off the track, lifting his feet through the rough grass. It was awkward for him, unnatural to his own way of moving. Amid the riot of emotions at seeing him, I realized he was truly a stranger here; 'not with the land' as the local farmers would have said. He was not 'with' the land at all, nor 'with' the sea, nor 'with' anything in this lonely place I had made so deep a part of myself. He was dark and strange and uneasy — and I loved him for being those things! I heard him mount the wooden boards of my verandah; sensed him standing there half-shy, half-amused. Surely my heart would burst! I opened the door. He looked bigger than I had remembered him. The varnished reflection of his checked shirt swung across me and into my cool house. I said straight out, not thinking:

"I don't even know your name."

"It's David. Hello. I thought

I would…"

"You've come to see me!"

"Well, yes. Elaine wanted to go riding today and frankly I'm scared of horses and I wondered if you sold your paintings. I was very impressed with the ones I saw the other day."

"That's very nice of you." How did I keep my voice so straight, so calm? "Please come in. My name is Susie Conrad."

He extended a warm hand and I shook it.

"I've never thought of selling them here," I said honestly. "Some of them get sold in London when I live there in the Winter. But you're very welcome to look through and take away as many as you like."

"No, I couldn't do that. I insist on paying. You *do* sell them?"

"Yes, but only in London. Like I said, I've never thought of selling them up here." I giggled away the years of my professional work, like a teenager admitting to an embarrassing hobby. "Nobody here knows."

"Then I do insist on paying."

"Okay. Well, have a look anyway. It's nice to meet someone who's interested."

Nice to meet him? My God, here he was coming into my house on the very day I could have died for want of him! How was I managing this? My whole body was tingling—worse than a girl on her first date. I watched him look me up and down, felt his eyes all over me, saw him glance again at my bare feet.

"I told you I never wear shoes here," I giggled again, "unless it's real cold or I'm going shopping in the village."

"By the way, how's the door?" He opened it again, peered into the varnish and gently touched its surface.

"The door is just beautiful." I closed it, saw him properly inside, then went to the store-room where I kept my paintings and drew out a portfolio. They had been done over the last two or three years, mostly coastal scenes, and I knew some were good. I was delighted that he wanted to look. "Have you quite gotten over your night on the desert island?"

"Yes, but only thanks to you."

"I knew Elaine was riding today." I made a show of sifting through the watercolours before I would let him see any of them. Did I sound too sly? I told myself I mustn't sound sly at all, mustn't let imagined guilt affect my voice. "Yeah—I met Jennie from the stables in the shop yesterday and Elaine was talking to her about the horses."

"Well I'm afraid horses and I don't get on. Being rubbed raw, thrown off, then bitten for good measure isn't my idea of a day out."

He meant me to laugh and I did.

"But Englishmen are supposed to love horses. Horses are noble creatures."

"Not the ones I've met—and I've had to meet plenty through Elaine. They're either vicious or plain daft; and I don't like driving without brakes."

"But you do have brakes: the reins, the bit, your signals to the horse."

"They've never read my signals very well."

"Okay, so we disagree about horses." I handed him the portfolio. "Perhaps we can argue about painting. Like a coffee while you're looking?"

"That would be very nice, thank you."

I made coffee for him, remembering the breakfast I had made for him after the rescue. But the girl had been with him that morning; today I felt like the only woman in the world.

"Where did you learn to paint so well?" He was studying the watercolors one by one.

"I used to be a stage-designer. I had to draw my ideas. Sometimes I had to color them in. I did it plenty and grew slick with it. But don't kid yourself, it's not Van Gogh."

"They look pretty good to me." He selected another painting. "A stage-designer, eh? How interesting. It's something most people never think about."

"That's how it should be. If

the audience notice it too much, it's probably overdone."

"Hmm. Was that in America?"

"Yes, and in London. I retired a long time ago."

"And came to live here?" He used a drawing to indicate the room.

"More or less."

"We live in Yorkshire, in Leeds. D'you miss London."

"No, not really. I miss the theater, though. I hardly ever go now, and don't really enjoy it when I do. I spend most of the play thinking I could do the set better."

"You probably could. Last time I went, the set was appalling." He selected another painting and looked at it, not at me. "Why don't you start up again? It must be marvellous to be creative."

"Oh, I'm out of things now. Nobody's going to hire me. I'm too old-fashioned and not famous enough for the big London companies, and starving with the hard-pressed provincials doesn't appeal. And creativity's probably overrated anyway. Remember, God gave it up after only six days." As I said this I wondered how much of my story I should tell him now, realized I had never said so many words in this house nor enjoyed myself so much — just by confessing these few facts of my life, so familiar to me, so new to him. "So — now I'm free to paint the best set of all," I nodded toward the window, "God's own."

He smiled. "The one He made in only six days, eh?" We both smiled. "Just think what else might have been out there if He hadn't taken that Sunday off. Okay — I'll have this one, and this one."

I sipped my coffee and looked.

"Mmm. Bamburgh Castle and Holy Island. You *would* find those two." I knew both were imperfect: Bamburgh altogether too pale; the causeway at Holy Island too stiff. "Sure as Hell you're not a painter."

"No, I'm an accountant."

"Ah — see an investment, do you?"

"No, I just like them."

"I could say there's no accounting for people's taste." This didn't get a laugh. "Okay, look. Bamburgh's the wrong color. You'd know that if you'd been there. And the one of Holy Island — it's just not as good as it should be."

"I don't care. I like them."

"I guess I can't argue with that."

"And," he held up my miniature of an oystercatcher, "I'll have this one as well."

"Ah. Now that *is* good, if I say so myself — and I just have, huh?"

"It's remarkable. I don't have to be a painter to see that. I like all your work. It's wonderfully clear and transparent — is that the right word? No, translucent. It must be the way you use the paint so thinly. It's very quick, isn't it, using watercolour?"

"Not necessarily. There's a lot of myth about the contrast with oils. It can be quicker than oil, but a good painting still takes a long time…and if you get it wrong in watercolor you can't fix it the same way you can with oil paint."

"But this one, the oystercatcher. Surely you couldn't have done it that small in oil. I mean it's almost like an engraving. The brushes you use…"

We talked on and on: about the work, the beach, the shape of the rocks, the sea-birds cutting the blue air, his job in Leeds, my life here. My little house — my tiny, lonely, cosy, desolate, dreaming, private world of a house — was filled for the first time with the simple, subtle joy of friendship. I bathed in it, revelled in it, danced with it. It was more precious and more wonderful and more beautiful even than my desire for him. That was hot and tingling in the very middle of me. I shamelessly longed for his arms around me, his hands over my skin, his mouth on mine, the heat of his love pouring around me, over me, into me. But the true wonder was the ease of our conversation, the genuine and unaffected glee of our togetherness, the give-and-take of words, the brew of speech and silence, the discovery of love as miraculous as water in the desert. Nothing was more wonderful than that…but it was spoiled by panic wriggling into me. I felt myself on the verge of tears and I held hard on to the chair to prevent myself from going on my knees to him, to beg from him his love, his affection, his understanding, his tolerance, even his pity. I was ready to do anything to keep him: anything from letting him tear off my clothes and take my body in any way he wanted to giving him my house and my open cheque-book. It was a horrible feeling, worse for being laughable—since I realized with perfect clarity that he didn't want my body, my house, my cheque-book, or anything else I might be able to give beyond my seaside hospitality and amiable chatter. He wanted his own life and he wanted Elaine. That was natural and right; it was pathetic and ludicrous that he should want me.

At last he made to go—completely innocent, I was sure, of my lust for him and of the devastating loneliness he would wreak upon me in the polite and cheerful moment of his leaving. He insisted on paying for the watercolors, unabashed by doing so: the only Englishman I've ever known who wasn't embarrassed by money. But I refused and he had to take them as a gift. I hoped, with an impure heart, that that he might say something like 'Well, I'll just have to find another way to repay you', but he didn't. He shook my hand again and joked about his reflection in the varnished door. For no other reason than to keep him a little longer and to bring him back, I said I would paint another picture especially for him. I saw he was surprised, pleased, perhaps even flattered. He accepted the idea eagerly as a kind of honor, but when he asked what the subject was to be I wouldn't tell him, making a great mystery of it, which I guessed he liked even more. The truth was I didn't know and didn't care. I was an ageing, lonely woman who wanted this handsome man back in her house. I wanted him to love me and I wanted him to make me happy again with his easysgoing conversation. He was young and strong and honest. I wanted him to love me, but I didn't want to trap him or ruin his life. I wanted a free run through every trick in the book—and if painting him a picture was a trick worth using, I'd use it.

8 The Show

Amazingly, after my harangue to Kaplin, everything began to go well for me on the show. Gavin made no more criticisms of my work and actually spent some time asking me how his actors should move through the wood and how they might best respond to the torn and muddied costumes I wanted in those scenes. The set went in on schedule without amendments and the Lighting Director finally turned on the sweet sunshine I had asked for. Most spectacular of all were the changes wrought in Mr. McHaddie the chief painter: as dour a Scotsman as ever grumbled his way over the Border. Everything had been a trouble to him, as if he had been dragged complaining from some Scotch mist still harboring a grudge about Culloden. Jack had met him in the theater and remarked with his usual cruelty that Mr. McHaddie would be the perfect man to give pep-talks to lepers. But McHaddie remained impervious to all jokes, however personal or nasty. He had gone about his business on the set like a monolith of dourness, making me feel it was my own fault that Shakespeare hadn't been born a Scotsman. Then suddenly he seemed to take me under his skeletal wing, muttering "Aye, ye've got the gleam aboot ye—the gleam, aye" and putting his crew of painters on their mettle. But this was not the limit of his enthusiasm. One night he caught me outside the theater and placed a bony finger on my lapel.

"Err—I've been wanting tae speak tae ye in private, Muss. Conrad."

"Oh, sure," I smiled. Whatever could it be? "Well, here we are."

"Err—would ye ever consider doing *Macbeth*?"

A terrible giggle rose in me but I defused it with a grin.

"Well sure I would, if the chance came along. It's a great play."

"Indeed. Indeed it is!" Mindful of superstitions about '*The Scottish Play*', he looked uneasily over his shoulder and drew me deeper into the shadows. I fought down my crazy chuckles. His manic vehemence subsided into a whisper of dreadful intent. "Remember what I tell ye tonight, Muss. Conrad. I'd be privileged tae paint ye the maist terrifyin' *Macbeth* ye'll ever see. Aye, once they put eyes on ma set, the people wouldnae be able tae sleep for fear o' being' murdered in their beds."

"That sure sounds something. I'll remember it, I promise."

McHaddie allowed himself a wintry smile, perhaps his only smile of the year.

"I would only undertake it for yeself, y'understand, if it was yeself who was the Designer, being sae specially talented a lady."

Suddenly I wasn't laughing at him any more, knew I should never laugh at him again, and couldn't resist putting my arms round him and kissing his withered cheeks.

"Mister McHaddie," I told him with a sniffle of tears in my nose, "reserve's for the English. What you've said to me tonight is the first thing that's really made me glad to be here and glad to be part of all this." I clung to his spare frame and found him stroking my hair.

"Och, ye shouldnae be grieving that they didnae understand ye. Ye're a rare woman wi' a vision all yer ain and already ye're making them see."

"Thank you, Mister McHaddie. " I straightened up and wiped my face. "Thank you from the bottom of my heart. You and me—we'll make this play the best thing they've ever seen and we'll show these fuddy-duddies and drama-school gooks what Shakespeare's all about, huh? And if I ever get to do *Macbeth*, I promise, I promise as sure as Hell, you'll be my chief painter. No," I kissed him again, "you'll be my co-designer!"

"Aye. Aye well." Unspoken sentiments bleared McHaddie's eye. "Will y'allow me tae get ye thus taxi?"

I allowed him to get me the taxi. Proud and flustered, he put me in it with all the ceremony due to a Queen of Scots and I was careful to thank him very graciously.

"Aye," he intoned through the window, "ye're a bonny woman of considerable talent—and mind that famous husband of yours looks after ye. Noo remember, ma *Macbeth* can haunt ye to the grave."

I was driven away, free at last to smile through my tears and sob with happiness.

* * *

"So, it's all coming right at last, is it?"

Richard was putting his finishing touches to the music track, editing a stately pavane to the right length.

"Yes, it's all coming right." I slid off my wooden-soled sandals, sat on his table and drank his coffee. I watched him work his magic over the heavy, huge-reeled recording machines, editing the tape with deft handling of marker-pencil, razor-blade and adhesive strip. If I had ever thought about it at all, I had imagined that music editing would be done by some amazing machine, not by a young man with a razor-blade and sticky tape. "You love your job, don't you?"

"Mmm." Richard was looking into the middle distance, listening for a beat in the music. I remembered his jokey boast that he could edit Beethoven's Ninth down to three minutes, quoting most of the themes and keeping a musical flow. "Mmm, I certainly do." Richard stopped the reel and marked the tape. "Did you know I do some freelance work in a recording studio? It's all good experience and you meet a lot of the groups. I met The Kinks the other night. They've got a great new record coming out. Yes, you're right, I love all this. How many people in London can wake up in the morning and look forward to going to work like we do?" He cut a length of tape and hung it round his neck. "Anyway, it looks like we all get to keep the jobs we love, thanks to your ding-dong with old Kaplin."

I put down my coffee.

"You heard about that?"

"Not half. It came down the grapevine like a fireman down a pole. We were all on your side of course—well, I think most of us were."

"I knew *you* were—though I still don't know why they resented me so much."

"Because you're American, because you're famous over there, because you have ideas of your own and stick to them and say what you think, because you were going to write your will across the stage in words of fire—or in your case *designs* of fire. Gavin thought it was all too much and squealed to Kaplin."

"But all those things you say I am and do, surely that's what they pay me for. Isn't that what they want? It's ridiculous!"

"The English are a ridiculous race." Richard smiled, stuck the tape together, and wound it back on the machine. "You must have noticed."

"I thought I'd cut my own throat by saying all that to Kaplin. I really did think he was going to fire me."

Richard pretended to sharpen his marker-pencil.

"Did you — er — did you ever take Jack's advice and apologise to Kaplin?"

"You heard about that as well?"

Richard shrugged another smile and made an eloquent gesture.

"We hear about everything down here, luv."

"Well, no, I didn't apologize. Should I have?"

"Obviously not. Kaplin probably loved being shouted at by a red-headed New Yorker who refused to apologise. Put a bit of passion in his life. Now he'll see you as the wild woman who turned his show on its head and made him a fortune. I'm sure he'll dine out on the story for years. Anyway, it paid off for you: you're virtually directing the show now…didn't you realise? Hell. Well for God's sake don't say *I* told you. And carry on directing anyway. Listen to this."

Richard clicked a button and his tape-machine began to play the pavane. The tiny room at the back of the stage was transformed into Shakespeare's golden garden, the Tudor rose bloomed once more, the sweet and melancholy wine of memory flowed again. I closed my eyes and laid my head on my knees. Why did Jack not love me as these people loved me: vibrant, rich and honest? They were full of endeavour and he was lazy. They were impassioned and he was careless. Why would he not be part of my triumph, set foot in the scented garden, step with me through the enchanted wood?

* * *

The days that followed could have been the happiest of my life. The sets and costumes were complete and rehearsals came to fever pitch. We all burned late into the nights—but on some evenings there was nothing more for me to do and I would come back to the flat and have a bath and lean out of the window into a wonderfully smokey London sunset: lights coming on, distant traffic, pigeons, black roofs and grimy brick, falling leaves, the sounds of children playing in strange and sooty gardens far below. The sun, huge and molten, poured its splendor over me, made me happy to my core yet yearn for things I could not name. I would think of Jack on stage as Higgins in another part of London, in another theater, in another life. We had not repaired our differences with much grace and had each retreated into our own work. There was something else, too: Jack was a great Higgins, but his play had settled into its run while mine was about to open. He was going to leave the cast for our two-week trip to Rome and an understudy would take over his rôle. The spotlight was shifting from him to me, and for all his apparently careless languor I suspected he was actually jealous. By quirks of circumstance opposite to those he might have imagined, and by the miraculous saving of her own brass neck, his wife was stealing his thunder. The ballyhoo for *Dream* was likely to be twice that for *Pygmalion* — thanks to my set, of course! — and suddenly the Press would be calling Jack my husband instead of me just his wife. He drank more and slept later and dirtied the bed and didn't care.

The opening party for *Dream* began in a fashionable restaurant and ended up in our flat. The first night had been an enormous success and we were all as high as kites. I had already heard the production described as a visual triumph and I knew I would get good reviews. Kaplin appeared at the restaurant and made a speech thanking everyone but looking at me. In an attempt at American wit — which someone must have written for him — he described me as a dame who didn't just bite the bullet but gnawed the bandolier as well. This got a laugh, I swigged off more Champagne, and felt vindicated. Happiest of all, Richard and Emma announced their engagement — to loud and drunken screams and plenty of ribald comments. Jack came in with a huge bouquet of flowers for me then hurried off home; in the taxi I gave the choicest blooms to Emma and Richard and cheered them on to longer and more passionate kissing. When we all rolled up to the flat Jack was there to meet us at the door, his arms full of Edwardian Champagne buckets. They were packed with ice and bottles and he served everyone as they came in. On the table they found boxes of Havana cigars and Swiss chocolates: his presents to the cast and crew for making my West End debut so successful. I was not at all embarrassed that Jack should treat me like a prima ballerina in front of these people. Everyone was happy and charmed by his generosity. It was old-fashioned and ostentatious, loud but sweet, and I loved him for it.

Much later, when morning light was creeping up and everyone was very tired and I was talking to Richard and Emma, Jack tugged at my arm.

"Sorry," I said to Richard as I was steered away. "Jack, what are you doing?"

"You've given my flowers away." Jack was rumpled and tired and the drink was settling him into

113

a stupor—but he could still manage a fizz of anger. "Well woman? You've given my bloody flowers away!"

"Two blooms, Jack: one for Richard and one for Emma. You know they're engaged."

"Who is that fellow?"

"He's Richard, the sound man. Remember? I told you all about him. He's the one who brought the show alive with all that marvelous music and the birds in the forest and the noises in the night. I owe him plenty."

Jack remained glum, then spat out: "He fancies you!"

"What nonsense. He's a very nice boy with a fiancée of his own age. I admire them both very much."

"Ah—so you fancy him back."

I smiled at Jack and was going to pat his arm—but suddenly he seized my wrists and grabbed at me.

"You fancy him, you tart!"

"Jack! People will hear us." I shook myself free. "For God's sake, he's twenty years younger than me. I'm old enough to be his mother."

"Doesn't matter. That'll not bother the likes of him. They're all loose, you know, loose as a sailor's arse...which reminds me, he's probably a poofta as well. Look at him; dressed up like an explosion in a paisley factory."

"Jack—I won't tolerate this from you. Now shut up and go to bed. You'll not ruin my party."

"*Our* party, my dear, *ours*. You see you're still not thinking like a wife. You really must give up these nancy-boys and learn to live with a real man. And I'm sorry to have to remind you—the real man in your life is me."

"Go to bed Jack. You can apologize when you've dried out."

He grabbed my wrist again. This time it hurt.

"You think I'm horrible, don't you? You're revolted by me, aren't you? That's the truth, isn't it?"

"No. The truth is that I love you—but nobody else will if you go on like this. Now go to bed, please. I'll come and be with you soon, okay?"

Jack swayed, considering my proposition. Then he lurched over to Richard, who at that moment happened to be holding a Champagne bottle.

"My wife's too old for you," he declared to an appalled silence. I was mortified with embarrassment: everyone could hear and see everything. "And anyway, she loves *me*. She's just said so, even though I am a bastard. Now I'll just borrow this." He wrenched the bottle from Richard and took a swig from it. "Don't worry, little poofta, you'll get it back—when I piss all over you."

* * *

A few days later, smart and sober and as handsome as a prince in a fairytale, Jack presented me with a beautiful cream-colored traveling coat with hat, shoes and handbag to match. He put me in the gleaming Bentley and drove us to the car-ferry at Dover, across

Europe and down long, hot, exciting roads to Rome. But I would never be able to love him truly again—not in the old, complete way.

9 The Painting

The beach is a place of mornings; even more so in the brief but dazzling Northern Summer. By noon the light has changed and the coastline—clear and burning through the brightest day—can wear a ravaged look. Smells and noises make their invasions; long evenings begin in early afternoon, night advances from the hills, the fresh day seems quickly done. If ever the world is made anew, it is on Summer mornings by the sea...and so it was on the day after David's visit.

I went out on to the verandah and found it bone-dry and hot beneath my feet. The sun was newly risen in a cloudless bowl and steeped my house in its brilliant yellow light. There was no breeze. Below, the sea was scarcely murmuring; above, the tiny silver arrowhead of a jet spewed out its long white tracery, perhaps en route for Iceland or Canada or traversing some polar Great Circle to the States. Its faint, distant roar might have been the very rolling of the Universe, a song between invisible stars. It folded like a silence over me; the shrill piping of the morning birds, wading and fluttering along the becalmed shore-line, seemed whispers in the shimmering air. Bathed in the glow of this wonderful morning, my senses alive to every note of its music, I was happy. The froth of my emotions worked a fine counterpoint to Nature's stately calm, and I was not cool or quiet. But I was happy.

My idea for David's painting had come with my awakening and was as brilliant as the sun that came so strongly on to my hands and face. I would paint this house, this house now sacred to our happiness. The best angle would be from slightly below the front, where the dunes began to fall away to the beach. There needed to be a fine billow of cloud behind the house, pure and dreamy, and a dramatic sense of silhouette, relieved by the sun's strong lighting across the verandah. It could only be done in the early mornings, when the sun came powerfully, as it did now, striping fiery edges to the planks and windows; not the soft, rich glow of evening, but the fierce new light of clear, unsullied day. It would also be the fierce new light of my new times with David. The effect I wanted would be difficult to achieve, especially if I put in that huge cloudscape: not a formation that came naturally in the mornings. But I would do it, bend every element to my purpose, use every advantage this place might give and stir in a few of my own. And the dramatic climax would be a reflection in that newly-varnished door: a reflection of myself actually painting the picture, lit glowingly by the same sun that was striking the house, but of course behind the viewer, looking into the picture with him, and out of it at him and myself: creator, observer and sharer of secrets. Like all the best tricks it was an old one, but I would do it anew from a fresh and gleaming angle, with all the subtle cheek

I could muster.

I set to work at once, downing my coffee and hurrying, half-dressed, over the grass and into the cool sand, looking at the house with new and critical eyes, sketching it roughly from different viewpoints but quickly finding the best one. As I marked the spot with a flat stone I realized I had never drawn or painted my house before. Starting the work was a very special moment. There and then in the early morning, kneeling on the coarse grass, carless of my uncleaned teeth and forgetting to comb my hair, I drew the outlines of the painting on a big new pad of heavy-grade paper. I had decided to paint this A2 size: larger than I normally used — but I wanted it to be big, bold and impressive, full of light yet packed with subtle detail too. The big paper size gave me new freedom, but was unfamiliar and daunting in a very exciting way: exactly how I wanted to feel about this new work. Carefully, slowly, I brushed the paper with my soft pencils. I could take my time over this—only the watercolors would have to go on quickly to capture the glimmering light of morning before a day of full sunshine took over. But that stage could wait. Right now I could take as long as I liked with the pencils. I sat an hour or more to the work, letting my mind roll with it.

David had gone from my house taking the promise of this painting, but we had fixed no time for his return. I should have organized that—but my nature has always been a strange mixture of the brash and the coy, of confidence and carelessness, of courage and cowardice. I could have made greater play for him, and I should certainly have arranged our next meeting, but I guessed that the very promise of the painting was its own assurance that he would be back. If the worst came to the worst I could deliver it to the farm, but that would defeat the advantage I had of bringing him naturally back to my house and would almost certainly involve meeting Elaine. She was still the unknown quantity. I examined my jealousy — and found it wasn't true jealousy at all. I simply wished she was not there, wished that David could have been as solitary and as lonely as myself, with a loneliness I might cure as he could cure mine. Yet even as I wished for different circumstances, I gloried in what had already come about; felt renewed and special in the sunlight, proud and chosen as the outline was completed, secure as I prepared my evening meal, protected as the Summer night breathed in from the golden countryside, drawing purple darkness across the sea and over my hot body waiting damp in its crevices from my throat to my knees as my mind sifted memories.

10 The Alps

On our way to Rome we stopped in Paris and broke our journey again with a few days at Innsbruck. I was surprised by Austria and loved it. Entering the brightly flowered valleys under the horns of snow to be welcomed by friendly and charming people: this was a spiritual homecoming, as if I had entered a dream in some forgotten cosy corner of my being. Warmth lay over the green land, bells intoned their stir of melancholy joy, pretty girls were selling flowers and soft music played in all the cafés. Yet the sharp heroic air woke me up to new appetites. Cool sunlight flooded the valley each morning as we breakfasted on rolls and coffee and thick sweet milk and special preserves of apricots and blueberries. We would go exploring in the colorful town with its red-shuttered houses and many-flowered window-boxes. Then we would drive up into the mountains, Jack nursing the long-nosed English car with delicate stirrings of his hands and feet, up into the blue and unfamiliar air, where clean sunshine seemed to come straight from Heaven and nut-brown mountaineers in green hats would salute us from the twisting roadside and we would stop at a tiny inn to lunch on venison stew and beef goulash and the bright white wine. We would scramble up narrow paths, rattling grey-green shards of stone beneath our feet and be rewarded, in a gasping sun-struck moment, with an eagle's view to Italy.

It was there, on the dizzy road's edge, I asked a passing mountaineer to take our photograph, handing him Jack's camera. He laughed and pointed and said things in German and turned us round to face the sun. It poured upon us in the full glory of the high Alps. I clasped Jack's arm and smiled beside him, remembering only how lovable he could be, how big and dark and strong and charming, and how the people at the hotel loved him too and had given us flowers for the bedroom and had been delighted when he'd kissed the *hausfrau's* hand in the Continental style and how even up here in cold air and hot sunlight he smelled of richness. The mountaineer clicked the camera and flashed us his gold-filled teeth and went on his way, whistling a tune and swinging his bare brown arms. Then we drove back down through scented woods and Jack bought me golden bracelets from the town. In the evening we danced to zithers and accordions in the hotel bar, eating many-layered chocolate cakes and peaches and grapes and drinking glasses of kirsch, and I would forget that there had ever been trouble and bitterness in London. I would try to forgive Jack completely, from the very middle of my soul, and think only of the sweet warmth of the valley at dusk and the soft white lacey quietness of our romantic wooden-walled bedroom and the blue and golden mornings and the great road snaking through the mountain passes running Southward to the long and lovely lakes, Southward ever Southward to the sun.

11 The Loving

I slept fitfully and woke early, hurrying to the door and stepping out quickly on to the verandah to check the morning. The planks were damp under my toes and a mist obscured the newly-risen sun, but the sky looked as if it would clear directly overhead. Given an hour, the morning might be just right for painting, so I went back in, made coffee and boiled eggs for breakfast and got the watercolors ready. But the mist, though thinning, was still there and the sun had yet to move up on to the house, so I put on a favorite jumper and skirt, tied up my hair in a scarf, and took a walk on the beach: along the soft sand, down to the hard cold beaten shore-line, daring to tolerate the chilly water round my ankles for the shocking wakefulness it always brought, then back toward the island.

It was strange to realize that I scarcely thought of David now I had begun a painting for him. I had two images of him: one in the boat as he watched me row, looking me up and down from my bare feet to my red hair; the other as he lifted the door to the blue sky and the rising music. They were beautiful, colorful, arrested moments, and I looked at them in my mind's eye over and over again, but with a satisfaction of having seen him rather than a yearning to see him again. Not yet, not until the painting was done, not until I could give it to him complete, perfect, and with love. The painting was for him, but he was not part of it; it was completely of myself and I knew I must be completely whole unto myself while it was being created. I turned some shells, looked in vain for round stones, watched a cormorant hang out its wings to dry on a rock at the back of the island...and realized that a full, warm, yellow sun was now streaming through the mist! I ran to the house, happy to the very middle of my being.

An hour later the house and the dunes were colored in: the same fierce light that I had seen and made part of my dream was now striped in orange paint across the paper. Even the fuzzy reflection of myself in the varnished door—tricky to do and liable to spoil the whole painting—had worked almost magically. There I was, sitting with one arm raising the brush. It all had the luminous effect I had longed to achieve. I was delighted with the result, returning through the morning to spend long minutes looking at it and not wanting to change one thing. Now all I needed was a golden evening with a mountain of cloud behind the house. I thought I might be given one this same day, but the early afternoon turned dull and rain drifted over from the hills: not the heavy showers which might have cleared to show the massive cumulus I wanted, but light and persistent rain from a solid gray sky. I shut myself in with a well-stoked stove and got busy cleaning the kitchen.

I wasn't thinking about David at all when he arrived. I had cans and crockery all over the room and was wondering how I put so much in so small a space when he knocked at my door. As I saw who it was, my heart leapt up again.

"Hello."

He was wearing a blue waterproof anorak and a canvas hat damp with the drizzle.

"Hi. Please come in. It's lovely to see you again. You've come for your painting, haven't you? Well, it's not ready yet; won't be long, though—another day or so."

Once again his presence had released a flood of words. I spoke so rarely to anyone. It was joyous to speak; to have him in front of me.

"Heavens, you've been quick," he said, taking off his hat.

"Would've been quicker if the sky had stayed clear. I need to see a particular type of evening cloud."

"It's a sunset, then?"

"Not exactly. You'll see. Are you very wet?"

"No, not really. The rain's easing off. You may get the cloud you want later on."

"Don't think so. I guess the rain's in for the day. Your coat can dry in front of the stove here."

He took it off and hung it, with his hat, on the back of a chair. It was very strange to have a man's things in my house. Even though I was excited by him and wanted him it was still strange, and he still the stranger.

"You certainly keep yourself busy," he remarked, eyeing the kitchen things piled on the table.

"Oh, there's always plenty to do when you live by yourself. Gotta keep the place clean — shipshape, as you British would say."

"I admire that very much. You're quite a lady, as you Americans would say." Did he know, in my smiling at him, how much he had excited me. "Can I help with all this?"

"No, no — let's have a coffee-break."

"It really is tea time."

"All these years in England and I still have *coffee*-breaks, okay?"

"Okay—but you must let me help you make it."

We laughed and made the coffee and sat beside the stove.

"Elaine's out riding again," he explained.

A stab of conscience went through me, but I forced myself to speak of her.

"Now that surprises me. Jennie doesn't usually take her horses out when it's raining like this: too much grooming to do afterwards."

He shuffled uncomfortably.

"Mm, but Elaine's mad keen, you know," he hurried on. "We were up in the hills yesterday, beyond Kirknewton."

"What, riding?"

"No, for a long walk." I knew the area, could see in my mind's eye the round green hills and brown moors, alive with birdsong and the distant cries of sheep. "We could see into Scotland; it was superbly clear." I imagined the view, wide and dreamy under warm, still skies. He told the story of driving up to the Border and the long sunny day he and Elaine had spent together. It came to me, quite suddenly while he was talking, that I must not interfere with this love and that my lust for him was perverse: the lust of an old and lonely woman for whom he could feel nothing but friendship, maybe even only tolerance. While he spoke of Elaine with love, he chatted to me like an old acquaintance...but that, of course, was part of his magic. I would control myself, finish the painting for him, cloud or no cloud, get it out of my house and get him out of my life. I had been stupid and selfish and I had to stop it now. "The best thing was, we saw the wild goats."

"Oh yes, I've heard about the goats." How was I able to make my chatter sound so calm, so casual? "Never seen them."

"Are they very shy?"

"I guess they are shy, yes, but it's not just that." Once more we were talking so happily we couldn't stop. "They live in a very remote area and they move around all the time. I've heard of people going up there for years and never seeing the goats. Plenty of sheep, that's for sure."

"Yes, I thought they were sheep at first, but they were in a rather peculiar huddle; I suppose that's what made me look in the first place. Then I realized they had long shaggy coats, brown and white—and there were one or two standing guard round the outside, with the mothers and the kids I suppose eating in the middle. Then one of them with horns—the Chief Billy, I suppose, if there is such a thing—he trotted out and looked right at us for a good few seconds. Then he led all the others off across the heather. Quite a sight, don't you think?"

"You've surely been very lucky." By now I was completely delighted by his story, warmed again by his boyish, innocent enthusiasm. "You really have been very lucky," I repeated.

"I know. It was as if I were being given something special, just for me." He fidgeted with his cup, a strange look in his eyes, as if he had been hurt. I saw it and he watched me seeing it, but I was going to admit nothing. He'd seen some wild goats and been impressed. So what? I didn't speak. "I've found something in this place," he went on.

"It's some place," I agreed quietly.

He put down his cup and stood beside me, over me. I went to jelly inside.

"Not that place; this place." Miraculously, wonderfully, gently and tenderly, he was stroking my hair. "And not anyone...you. Not anyone but you."

"I'm too old."

I said it blunty, coldly, even though the soft pressure of his hand was warm and wonderful and I never wanted him to stop caressing me. He didn't say 'No you're not', which I expected. He said: "You're never too old to be in love."

It was true, of course, as true as the years that should have made all this impossible, but I hated the trite sound of its generous wisdom, hated and loved it all at once.

"How long did you rehearse that one?"

I wanted to be cruel, to stop this now. But he would not be hurt or stopped any more than I could keep on denying the shivers of desire running through me with every stroke of his hand.

"Funny," he said—and I knew he was smiling even though I did not look up—"it just came to me."

I let him stroke my hair in silence, did not move, let tears run from my eyes. With the skill and gentleness and control of a much older man he dabbed my eyes with a handkerchief. So young men still carried handkerchiefs? I half smiled at my own surprise...and still he stroked my hair to the warm hiss of the stove and the light splash of rain from the eaves. With a motion I knew would change everything, I reached for his other hand and drew it to my lips, looking up at last and into his face. He was kissing me...softly, with a dry, featherlight touch I had not expected and had never known;

pushing my shirt off my shoulders and taking his lips gently around my neck and throat. It would not be long, I thought, before our relationship would cross a border into a new country where we would become new people and from which—because of the simplest, oldest, most natural actions in the world—there would be no coming back. He was gentle, but he was sure; tender, but inexorable...and now my breasts were bare. In the middle of it all I wished for a younger, firmer body and wondered what he would make of the lines and sags his fingers must have crossed already. But he whispered something like my name, as if uttering a prayer to sanctify this station of the rites beween us. He licked my skin— not wildly or wetly, but with the tiny tip of his tongue. I didn't know if this was a regular man's trick, but I'd never had it done before and I gave myself up to its new and simple wonder. Then he came down on me with his hot mouth open and he kissed me hard and full. "Oh, David, if you kiss me like that…if you kiss me like that…" I moaned and arched my body but he made no sound; he went on kissing my breasts and my throat and my breasts again. "David, if you kiss me like that…" With my own hands I opened his trousers and tore at my skirt. He was quiet and gentle and went on kissing me and stroking my skin but I stripped myself under him, wantonly splitting the pale cotton of my skirt, tearing it away, and with it all the long and unloved years of my life, baring my thighs about him, curving my whole body up and into and around his and relaxing into love with him: long and strong, slow and sweet, wild and tender. And in the sleep that fell about me I dreamed of bright flames.

12 The Candles

It was the return trip from Rome and I was driving—driving mechanically with a pain in my heart and tears in my eyes and Jack still asleep in the car beside me, still drunk after a party in Milan. He hadn't wanted to leave so early that morning but I'd known we had to get back to London and that if we didn't start early we would miss our pre-arranged stop in Paris and our Channel-ferry the next day. So I'd eaten breakfast, dragged him out of bed, piled him into the car, and with curt goodbyes to his friends we had set off Northward for the Alps and the long French roads. He had eaten nothing but he'd still been sick all over his beautiful car and now he was heavily asleep with a dampness on his brow and a wetness at his lips.

Low on petrol, I stopped the Bentley in a village, deep and quiet in the Austrian farmlands. The arrival of a big foreign car was still an event here. While the garage man fussily filled the tank and ordered his son to check the engine and the tyres and to clean the windshield with a plastic-handled sponge, I wandered off to stretch my legs and sniff the warm, fresh, morning air.

A few steps down the road stood a little church. I strolled idly up to it, found the newly-painted door enticingly ajar, and went inside. A froth of candy-colored plaster enveloped me in its happy European vision of Heaven, rosy baroque paintings spread behind the altar and vases of flowers stood on every windowsill, filling the place with a freshness like Mozart. I relaxed, feeling elated and content at the same time.

Good and simple people came in here each day to tend the flowers and to pray. They lit candles to their saints and went out across their fruitful fields beneath the changeless peaks of snow. A rack of burning candles was proof that there had been such visitors this very morning; now I had come into their quiet church, the smells of sin and sorrow on my clothes, and it had welcomed me no less warmly. Outside, in vibrant sunshine beating through the door, Jack would be snoring under fuddled memories of Milan, already miles behind us in an unrevisitable past. I felt I had driven into a new dimension where Jack was simply an encumbrance: coarse and careless and unable to help himself or return my love. Maybe it was neither his fault nor mine, or maybe we were both to blame, but it would go on for ever unless I stopped it.

I walked slowly to the candles, lit one, and held it up before me. Its blue and yellow flame was pure and lovely, innocent and sacred. I lit it for my sins and for the sins of Jack, to whom I could give no more love and from whom I would go as soon as I could. The resolve to leave him didn't cancel out the love I had once borne him, for somehow, in the flame's bright halo, that love was illuminated and I saw the brief wonder we had shared. But the flame also consumed the last of that old love and threw no line to rescue it. It showed me a new truth: henceforward I would be my own woman. Here, in the heart of the old Europe so far from my birthplace but to which some secret part of my soul was forever turning, I began to live my own life. Then I lit a second candle from the first: this was for Richard and Emma, embarked on some joyous honeymoon of their own, and whose love was not sullied by drink or bitterness and who deserved bright candles lit for them around the world.These revelations were simple, eloquent and innocent. I was glad they had come to me in a church, especially one so beautiful and so calm. If I could have stayed there all my life I think I might have done so — looking through the door at an eternity of dawns and sunsets, lazing through the mellow Summer days, sheltering from icy Alpine storms, awakening to the Spring-green fields. But I knew that could not be, so I lit a final candle and made a vow: if I fell for another man, not to fall too far and lose my identity somewhere beneath him; to love, but not to resign. That candle was for my future: for whatever might happen beyond this blue and golden day which surely could not just be an end but must—as certainly as morning—be a beginning for new honesty and new courage: the courage to walk away from candles, out of the shadow and into the sun.

13 The Truth

It was like waking to a new life. I realized I didn't love him. He was young and handsome and he had brought me to this—but I didn't love him. I loved Jack—or the magic of what had been Jack before drink and bitterness had destroyed it. I loved everything I had done in the theater and I loved my solitary life in this little house beside the sea. And that was all I loved. That was all I would ever love. This young man relaxed upon my naked body was an interloper, an aberration, a clearing of my throat in a song he couldn't sing. He was a stranger, I was a fool. It was my new life but I was no different and could be no different...only now perhaps I would be more honest with myself—and with him. I rolled stiffly from David's arms. He continued to sleep on the floor. The rain had stopped but the afternoon was darkening to a gloomy evening. I looked at my torn skirt with disgust and crept naked into the bathroom. I didn't feel beautiful or fulfilled or any of the things he would like me to say I felt. I felt tired and impure. I told myself all this had been inevitable from the moment I had dared to let him into my lonely life, but also that it didn't have to go on for ever. A kind of madness had passed over me leaving...nothing at all. In the emptiness I could find no meaning or purpose, just a sense of loss and waste and betrayal. 'Once you've climbed over the orchard wall,' went the old Yiddish saying, 'you might as well steal the fruit.' But the fruit was bitter and bruised from the grasp of my own hands. I had climbed the wall with plain intent; now I didn't want the fruit at all.

When I came back in a new skirt and blouse David was leaning against the window. I went straight up to him, smoothed his hair less tenderly than he had stroked mine, and said:

"I'm sorry."

It was a genuine apology, but I was equally sorry for myself. He was wide awake and looked happy. I was going to ruin it all for him.

"Don't be sorry," he answered, making to kiss me, but I held his hands away.

"I am though. I'm sorry I've done this with you and I'm sorry for Elaine."

His face clouded and stayed that way. I carried on.

"You know I can't say I didn't want this to happen because I did—and you know I did. But it was a big mistake. I wish it hadn't happened for your sake and for Elaine's—and for mine."

"Elaine doesn't know about this."

"Maybe she should. Maybe you should tell her about what happened here, if you have the guts. If you haven't, keep schtum and hope she never finds out, huh?"

"I can't tell her. She'd find it impossible to understand, impossible to forgive."

"Maybe it is impossible to forgive. Anyway, that's why I'm sorry and why this mustn't happen again."

147

"That's ridiculous."

"Not as ridiculous as an old woman with a young man."

"Look—you've got to forget this nonsense about your age. Your age doesn't matter to me."

When I made no reply he became hectic.

"You can't deny you wanted me!"

"No I can't deny that and I won't. But my age *would* start to matter to you and you'd fall out of love with me. So, because neither of us can tell Elaine or be understood or forgiven, I want you to go back to her and not deceive her or any of us any more."

"I've tried to be honest," he said. His big frame and his handsome face carried the lies well. A younger woman would have believed him—but I came in for the kill.

"Then why didn't you tell me the truth about where Elaine is today? I know she's not riding; Jennie doesn't take the horses out when it's raining as hard as this. She just never does."

As he shrugged in the trap I had made for him I knew I sounded blunt and schoolma'amy. Then I thought his admission too quick, too easy, like one given just to gain credibility.

"Yes, you're quite right. I shouldn't have tried to fool you, knowing this place as you do. We argued. She took the car and went shopping — in Berwick, I think."

"And what did you argue about? Was it me by any chance?"

"Yes it was. I told her I was going to buy a painting from you."

"And what did she say to that?" He stood mutely. "Come on, give."

"Well, she said I should be spending time with *her* on holiday instead of going to see…going to see a lonely old woman." As an apologetic afterthought he added: "I'm sorry, but you did ask."

"No, no, don't be sorry. She was quite right."

"I don't think of you like that. Those were *her* words."

"They were the right words."

149

"How can you say that?" he was pleading and fighting at the same time. "How can you, after today?"

"Because it's the truth, David. I *am* a lonely old woman. What neither you nor Elaine accept is that I'm quite happy to be one—and to face the truth. I've lived alone so long I've grown used to the truth. It's only other people who make you lie. The truth is so simple. It might be hurtful sometimes but it's beautiful. It's easy too: if you always tell the truth you never need to remember anything. That's Mark Twain, by the way. You want to try it some time."

"Why did you do it then? Why did you lead me on in that way?"

"Oh, so it's all *my* fault now, huh?"

"Just tell me why."

Tears stood in my eyes.

"Okay. It was because I hadn't known love for so long," I almost sobbed, "from anyone, for so long…for so long…"

He was going to be tender,

he was going to put his arms around me—but I wasn't going to let him. He couldn't understand why I was rejecting him and passing up what must have looked like a good chance. He wouldn't understand until years later, wouldn't see it was for the sake of his own freedom, and mine.

"And because I've started to tell you the truth I'll have to tell you all of it. It's about how I live and how I want to go on living." I dried my eyes. "I've made a special life for myself up here. Some folks might think it's strange and lonely and I guess in some ways it is but, amazingly, I like it. I like it a lot and I don't give a damn what anyone thinks or says about that. You believe I'm giving you up just because you're years younger than me. Well, that's one reason, I suppose. I say giving you up; hey, I haven't even taken you on! What I mean is, this age thing isn't the main reason. Really it isn't. When people are completely in love it doesn't matter what age they are. But you and I aren't completely in love—how could we be? We don't know enough about each other. No, it's all down to the real person I am. I need love as much as you do—maybe even more, and I don't mean that to sound arrogant. It's for reasons in my past you just don't know—and think yourself lucky you don't. But the sort of love I need, you just can't give me. Hell, that sounds so cruel! This is all down to me, not your fault. You can't know the things I've been through with my husband and my career and why I don't want just sex any more. I loved my husband Jack. For just a short while I loved him with everything I had and now, although I left him years ago, I love the memory of what he was. I loved my work in the theater and now I love painting here and this little house and my lonely life in it...and that's all I love, David. Sex just can't be enough. I know what I allowed to happen today was wrong of me, but I just couldn't resist you. You are a lovely lover. Be pleased about that. I thought I was fulfilled, or if I wasn't, that you would fulfil me. But as you get older you realize you're not fulfilled at all. You've got less and less time to do what you really want and need to do."

"So," he was all ready to be angry again, "what do you really want and need to do?"

"Just to go on as I am, living here, painting when I feel I have to."

"Nothing else? Nothing at all?"

"Not unless it comes naturally to me."

"Like me, I suppose. I've 'come naturally to you', have I? So you'll have your bit of fun and throw me out afterwards as if nothing has happened."

"That's terribly unfair."

"But it's the truth, isn't it?" he growled. "You're supposed to like the truth."

"Okay, think that if you want to. Think that if it helps you to hate me and drive you back to Elaine. That's where you belong, not with me. I thought for a crazy moment that loving you could be part of my life, but it just can't be.

I'm sorry if I hurt you, but there is just no way you can be part of my life. Elaine's right. I'm a lonely old woman. I know myself too well — but you mustn't think I'm unhappy; you mustn't think you can come to some romantic rescue. I'm fine as I am. I'd only make you more unhappy than you are right now."

"Even though you started it?"

"That is so *childish*! But yes, even so."

He couldn't understand me at all. He looked as if he might be going to explode. He actually clenched his fists like a frustrated toddler.

"You're going to destroy everything that's been made in this...this magic?" Now he did not seem childish. Now he seemed to speak pure poetry. "You're going to turn away the gift?" How eloquent, I thought. How fortunate, in the most dreadful moments, to have the power to find such words. And I nodded and stood aside.

"I reckon you'll be happier

when you're back with Elaine."

He was silent and immobile. His eyes asked: 'Do we not even part with a kiss, not even one kiss after all this? Do I not even take away a sweet memory of my woman who lived by the sea, who so needed my love? Can we not even be kind to each other, not share some love in a rotten world?' And my eyes answered: 'No.'

"You're beautiful," he said, "but you're hard. You're a hard woman."

"Your turn in the bathroom," I said.

* * *

Evening at the edge of the sea. The air was warm and still. Big clouds had ridden up with the late afternoon and stood like mountains in the Southern sky, bathed in sunlight more perfect than a saint's vision. Distant songbirds whistled across the farmland, their sounds mingling with the quiet folding of the water. The painting lay on its board, propped up on the verandah, but I could not bring myself to finish it — not until I had calmed myself and made new peace between my body and my soul. I stood in my long-familiar pose at rest against the rail and looked down across the beach. I was a woman who lived by the sea. The tides would roll, the sun would burn above me, the sea would whisper below. There was a sanity and a wonder in that. I felt that if I could only fall back into the rhythm of my old life, absolved and unconscious, then I might once again know happiness.

A girl appeared along the beach. It knew it was Elaine by the bright hair and slender figure. She came slowly, idly; her thin arms dangling from her striped jumper, her long legs in white jeans cut short above the ankle so her pale feet could paddle along the water's edge. Every so often she would stop, turn a shell with her toes, bend down and pick up a pebble to throw out to sea, or stand looking at the horizon and back into the dunes. I shrank into a shadow.

From the opposite direction came David, running easily along the sand in pair of shorts. His body looked hard and dark and when he came up to Elaine he stopped running and she seemed paler and thinner beside him. They embraced loosely, their feet in the sea, and he bent down to spatter her with a handful of water. She squealed and laughed and pretended to run away from him but it didn't last long and they were together again, walking out into the little waves, wetting her jeans, turning them a darker color, stretching their arms for balance now they were up to their thighs in the water.

'I'll go back to the Alps and light a candle for him,' I thought, 'high in a little church surrounded by blue air. I'll marry him in spirit and sanctify the memory of him and ask forgiveness for my sins, just as I did with Jack.' But then I thought: 'No, I can't. The candle lit so long ago is now burned out, such marriages are girlish dreams, such memories are profane, and

157

such sins exact more terrible penance.'

Gentle waves rolled up to their waists and left them again. They kissed. She stroked his arms. They stood against the light, caressing hair and faces.

'I'll treasure the painting I have done for him,' I thought. 'It has distilled our joy as purely as the photograph with Jack in the Alps distilled my joy with him, as purely as the Enzian schnapps we drank in those far mountains distilled the spirit of the blue gentian flowers.' But then I thought: 'No, my greatest skills are powerless to portray this wonder; all the candles of Europe would be a pale gleam against the fire I am watching.'

He put her arms above his head and pulled off her jumper, threw it carelessly back to shore, cupped his hands and poured water over her gleaming shoulders. It ran from her breasts, bare beneath the sky. I saw that I was past the age to go bare-breasted. She held out her arms to him. My arms were suntanned and wrinkled and the flesh sagged from them while hers were pale and smooth and firm. I was past the age to play with cool water beneath an evening sun. I watched them in the water and knew my loss was their gain, my end their beginning. I was a woman who lived by the sea. The tides rolled, the sun burned above me and the sea whispered below. The people made no difference to that—except this once. I knew, when the chips were down, that I could not be relied upon to be anything but selfish. He reached into the water as if to catch something swift and difficult to hold—and drew up a strand of seaweed. I could see it, green and glistening, even from my verandah. He hung it about her throat like a mermaid's necklace. I reached into the shadows and took up the painting, tore it in half, and again, and again. I recalled that vow I had made in the Alpine church: to love, but not to resign. Then, with a new sense of freedom and contentment, I went back inside my house and closed the door.

The End

About the Author

Poet, novelist and scriptwriter Roger Harvey was born in 1953 and lives in Newcastle. He took a degree in Law and became a teacher of English, History and Drama before establishing his career as a writer. He has written many works for radio and is one of Britain's most published poets. Among his poetry collections are *Raising the Titanic*, *Divided Attention*, *How Happy Were the Mornings* and the award-winning audio-book *Northman's Prayer*. His published plays include *Asra! Asra!*, revealing the secret love-life of Samuel Taylor Coleridge, the black farce *Money! Money! Money!* and the pantomines *Up the Pole* and *Donkey Skin*; after its stage tour his play *Guinevere-Jennifer* was made into a film. *Poet on the Road* is the intimate travelogue of Roger's reading-tour across the U.S.A. and *The Writing Business* a miscellany of essays on the literary life. His novels include *The Silver Spitfire*, *Percy and Dinah*, *The White Owls of Winter*, *Maiden*

Voyage, set around the building of the transatlantic liner *Mauretania,* and *Room for Love* with its sequels *Room for Me* and *Room for Us.* Among his other books are the nostalgic children's adventure *Albatross Bay,* the romantic comedy *River of Dreams* and the short-story collection *The Green Dress and Other Stories.* Roger is married to Sheila Young, an expert on Royal jewellery whose book *The Queen's Jewellery* became the definitive work on the subject. His other interests include music, photography and classic cars. For further information please visit RogerHarvey-writer.blogspot.com

Printed in Great Britain
by Amazon